THE MESSAGE IN THE HOLLOW OAK

A group of professional detectives challenge Nancy to tackle a mystery that they have failed to solve: find an invaluable message hidden by a missionary centuries ago in a hollow oak tree in Illinois.

While searching the woods for the ancient tree, Nancy and her friends live with a group of young archaeologists who are excavating prehistoric Indian burial mounds on a nearby farm. A shadowy enemy stalks Nancy and harasses everyone at the dig. The young investigator pursues her dangerous adversary to an outlaws' cave, and is threatened when she discovers an unusual treasure.

How Nancy, with few clues to go on, solves this complex mystery will thrill all readers.

The car balked at the rocks

NANCY DREW MYSTERY STORIES

The Message in the Hollow Oak

BY CAROLYN KEENE

NEW YORK

Grosset & Dunlap

PUBLISHERS

Contents

CHAPTER I

Indian War Secret

"NANCY," said the voice on the telephone, "you are wanted in New York City!"

The eighteen-year-old girl detective looked a bit startled. Was this a joke? Or true? "Why, Aunt Eloise, what for?"

Eloise Drew laughed at the apprehension in her niece's voice. "For a mystery," she replied.

Nancy relaxed. "Oh! For a moment you had me scared. Your announcement sounded as if I was being brought up on some police charge." Then she added, "Tell me about the mystery. That's more to my liking!"

To Nancy's disappointment, her aunt said it was too long a story to explain over the phone. "I was calling to see if you would like to visit me and meet a friend of mine, a detective. He wants some help on a baffling case."

Nancy's pulse quickened. She was only an ama-

1

teur detective. How could she possibly assist a man with professional training and ability in capturing criminals?

"Aunt Eloise, please tell me more!" Nancy pleaded, rumpling the reddish-blond hair that framed her attractive face.

"No, I'll leave that to my friend. His name is Boyce Osborne. All I can say is that the case involves a trip to Illinois."

"It sounds interesting," Nancy replied. "I'll have to ask Dad if he has made any plans for me this weekend."

Her aunt laughed again. "We're one step ahead of you. He has already given his permission for you to come. Can you be here some time tomorrow afternoon?"

"Yes," the young detective answered. "See you then, Aunt Eloise."

Nancy hung up. She was excited at the thought of a puzzling new case to solve. Going into the Drews' cheerful living room, she exclaimed, "Well! The things that go on behind my back!"

Carson Drew, a prominent lawyer in River Heights where he and Nancy lived, glanced up from his paper. He was a tall, handsome man who had been a widower since Nancy was three years old.

Seeing his daughter's teasing expression, he relaxed. "Going visiting?" he asked.

"Of course," she replied. "Have you ever known

me to turn down a mystery? Maybe Bess or George will drive me to the airport tomorrow."

Bess Marvin and her girl cousin George Fayne were Nancy's closest friends and she was eager to tell them about her latest assignment. She secretly hoped that somehow they could be included in it.

Nancy hurried to the telephone and called the two girls. Both of them were excited at her news and agreed to take their friend to the airport.

After hanging up, Nancy went to the kitchen to tell the housekeeper, Mrs. Hannah Gruen, about the trip to New York. The motherly woman, who had taken care of Nancy since the death of Mrs. Drew, smiled. "Please give your aunt my warmest wishes," she said.

"I certainly will," Nancy replied.

The following noon Bess and George arrived. Bess was a slightly plump blond with delightful dimples. George, in contrast, was very slender and athletic looking and wore her dark hair short. Both of them had on casual summer dresses.

"Oh, Nancy, you look neat!" exclaimed Bess as she and her cousin admired the young detective's smart beige suit.

After saying good-by to Hannah, they drove at once to the River Heights airport and Nancy hurried off to catch her plane to New York.

By midafternoon she was entering her aunt's apartment house. To Nancy's surprise the elevator was no longer manned. A self-service car had been installed. It was standing open. She walked in and pushed the fourth-floor button.

The door closed and the car slowly started upward. Halfway between the second and third floors it stopped suddenly. The next moment the lights went out.

"Oh dear!" thought Nancy. "The power is off!"

She took a flashlight from her purse and beamed it on the bank of buttons near the door. She pushed one marked "Emergency," but it did not ring.

"Now what am I going to do?" she asked herself. "Without power, there's no way of moving this car."

Nancy waited several minutes for the electricity to come back on, but nothing happened. She began to pound on the door. Surely someone would hear the noise and investigate. But no one did.

Nancy decided to shout. "Help! Help! I'm stuck in the elevator!"

It seemed to her like a very long time before there was any response. Then faintly she could hear a man's voice.

"I've been ringing for the elevator. There must be a power failure. Where are you?"

"Between the second and third floors," Nancy called. "Please get me out!"

"Hold on!" the man yelled back.

There was silence for the next ten minutes and Nancy became disheartened. Had the man gone

Nancy shouted, "Help! Help! I'm stuck in the elevator!"

off and failed to keep his promise? How long would she be a prisoner?

Finally the stranger called loudly, "Can you hear me?"

"Yes," Nancy responded. "Is somebody going to start the elevator?"

"I'm afraid not," he called back. "I reported this to the superintendent and he called the elevator company. There's nothing they can do. It's a power failure in this part of town. You'll just have to be patient."

Nancy stifled a groan. "Just as I was about to find out about my new mystery!" she said to herself. Then she thought of her aunt and Boyce Osborne. They would be wondering what had become of her.

"Are you still there?" she shouted.

"Yes."

"I'm Nancy Drew and I've come to visit my aunt, Miss Eloise Drew. She lives on the fourth floor. Would you mind going to her apartment and telling her what happened?"

"I'll do it at once," the man promised.

By this time the superintendent had come and other tenants on the third floor had gathered. There were exclamations of "You poor thing!" "Keep your chin up." "I think this is terrible."

In a few minutes a welcome voice called down. "Nancy?"

"Aunt Eloise!" How relieved Nancy felt!

"Honey, I'm so sorry this had to happen, but I'm sure we'll have you out of there in a little while."

Nancy and her aunt kept conversing and occasionally the neighbors, and even Boyce Osborne, came to lend encouragement. An hour went by. Then suddenly the lights in the elevator came on and with a sigh of relief Nancy ascended to the fourth floor.

Aunt Eloise greeted her niece with open arms. Miss Drew, a schoolteacher, was tall and lovely looking. She led the girl to her apartment and introduced her to Boyce Osborne who had gone back.

"Call me Boycey, as everyone else does," he said, shaking Nancy's hand. The detective was of medium height. Although he was rugged looking, the man had a very kind face and Nancy thought his smile was enchanting. How different from many comic-strip detectives!

"I'm looking forward to working with you," Nancy said. "Do tell me about the mystery we're to solve together."

Boycey smiled. "Not together," he told her. "You are going to solve it yourself."

Nancy's eyes opened wide. "Alone?" she asked.

Aunt Eloise spoke up. "Suppose you two talk things over while I prepare dinner."

After she had left the room, Boycey Osborne selected a chair next to Nancy's. "First I must tell you that a group of us detectives have a sort of club. We take our vacations together at the same time every year and compete with one another in solving a mystery. Recently we returned from Illinois, defeated. When I told your aunt about it, she immediately laughed and said, 'I'll bet my niece could find the message in the hollow oak.' "

"The message in the hollow oak?" Nancy asked, puckering her forehead.

"Here is the full story," Boycey began. "Our club's so-called fun mystery this year turned out to be more baffling than tracking down a criminal. In the river country area around Cairo, Illinois, there is a certain legend about a French missionary from Canada named Père François. He is supposed to have hidden a message of great importance. He had been traveling from village to village, converting Algonquin Indians.

"Then suddenly the powerful Iroquois swarmed down and nearly annihilated them. This was in 1680. Père François escaped but he had been wounded by an arrow. Later he was found unconscious by a pioneer many miles from the battle scene. He was nursed by this man and regained consciousness only long enough to say, 'Valuable message in hollow oak.' Then he died."

"A sad story!" Nancy commented. "What makes you think the secret message wasn't found or that the hollow oak hasn't long since been blown over and disintegrated?"

Boycey smiled. "I can see that you are a practical young lady with a logical mind."

Nancy blushed a little at the compliment and said, "Perhaps I inherited these traits from my father. But tell me more of your story. Why did you and your friends give up the search?"

"For one thing, we used up all our vacation time and had to return here," he responded. "But we did make a little headway. Apparently Père François wanted to leave a record of the Indian villages he visited. We found a hollow oak which had blown over. On the trunk was a bulging area which we cut away.

"Underneath the bark was a lead plate with the name Père François and the date 1675. Below it was an arrow. There was nothing inside the trunk. Some of us figured out which direction the arrow had originally pointed. We took an easterly course, but before we could locate another hollow oak, it was time for us to go for our plane and fly home."

"I'm amazed," said Nancy, "that a tree three hundred years old and hollow in 1675 would have survived all this time."

Boycey told her that oaks are very sturdy trees and have been known to live for many centuries so it was not surprising to find one three hundred years old. "By the way," he added, "the oak is the state tree of Illinois."

The detective leaned forward in his chair and

asked, "Would you like to finish the case my friends and I had to abandon?"

Nancy's eyes danced with excitement. "Right now I can't think of anything I'd rather do more."

"Good!" Boycey said. "And I wish you all the luck in the world."

Aunt Eloise announced dinner was ready. During the meal, the conversation continued about the message in the hollow oak.

"It certainly sounds interesting," Miss Drew commented. "Boycey, I just want to ask you one question. Do you think it will be perfectly safe for Nancy to go to that area and undertake a search?"

The detective took several seconds before answering the question. Finally he said, "There's one thing which perhaps I should warn you about. We detectives had a little trouble with a man named Kit Kadle. He's eager to find the message himself and told one of my friends he wouldn't let anything stand in his way of getting it!"

CHAPTER II

Annoying Traveler

AUNT Eloise put down her forkful of roast beef and looked intently at her niece.

"Nancy, I don't like the sound of this man named Kit Kadle. If he's so eager to find out what the message in the hollow oak is, he may be dangerous. I can't imagine that he would let a girl outsmart him, and if you should succeed, he would be right there to harm and rob you."

"Oh, Aunt Eloise, aren't you painting a much worse picture than the way things really are?"

Boycey Osborne answered. "Eloise, I'm afraid you are. I was merely telling Nancy to keep her eyes open in case this Kit Kadle should still be around. He may have given up the search, just as my friends and I did."

"Perhaps you're right," Miss Drew conceded. "Anyway, it would be your father, Nancy, who would make the decision about your going."

The girl detective nodded. She realized Aunt Eloise wanted to protect her, but not necessarily stop her from the fun of solving another mystery.

Many times before, friends had tried to dissuade Nancy from pursuing the work she loved so much. She found each new mystery intriguing and was always impatient to start solving it. This had been true from her first adventure, *The Secret of the Old Clock,* to the previous one, *The Clue of the Broken Locket.* Now Nancy could not wait to get to southern Illinois and begin work on her new assignment.

Boycey said, "I'm sorry I brought up Kit Kadle's name. So far as I know he is merely overaggressive and doesn't play the game fairly. But I wouldn't say he's dangerous."

The detective now brought a map for her from his pocket. In one place there was a big red X. He explained that this was the spot where he and his friends had found the hollow oak.

"Here are pictures." He produced snapshots which showed the stump with hundreds of age rings and also the fallen tree among some bushes a short distance away. The section he had gouged to uncover the lead plate could be seen clearly.

"Whenever the bark of a tree is removed or disturbed," he explained, "a new surface gradually appears to heal the wound."

Suddenly Boycey Osborne snapped his fingers. "I just thought of something. In the general area where this oak is there's a dig going on. It's under the auspices of the Archaeological Department of Paulson University and is open to students. The name of their leader is Theresa Bancroft. The girls in the group are staying in a rented farmhouse with Miss Bancroft. The boys live in another old house about half a mile away.

"I'm sure the girls would let you room with them. The only trouble is it's very difficult to get in touch with Miss Bancroft. She has no telephone and doesn't go to town very often to pick up mail."

Nancy thanked him for the information, thinking, "If I can't contact the leader, I certainly can't stay there." But she said nothing to the others.

At ten o'clock Boycey announced he must leave. He gave Nancy a warm handshake.

"Just concentrate on the mystery," he said, "and I'm sure you'll solve it somehow." He grinned. "Wait until I tell my friends a girl found the message in the hollow oak!"

Nancy chuckled. "I hope I won't disappoint you, but I realize you've given me a really big job."

Aunt Eloise remarked that it would be a miracle if Nancy could solve the mystery with so few clues to go on. Her niece agreed.

The following morning, after attending Sunday church services with her aunt, she left for home. Mr. Drew was away, but Hannah Gruen greeted her and wanted to know at once what the new mystery was.

When she heard about it, the housekeeper shook her head. "I'm sure your father will never agree to this Illinois trip, unless friends are with you."

Hannah was right. When Nancy made the proposal to Mr. Drew that evening, he shook his head.

Seeing the look of utter disappointment on Nancy's face, he said, "When your Aunt Eloise asked me if you could work on this case she didn't mention you would be by yourself. She probably didn't know. It would be too dangerous for you alone, Nancy. But if Bess and George can accompany you, I'll give my consent."

The next minute Nancy was on the phone talking to Bess and telling her about the mystery.

"How exciting!" Bess exclaimed. "But what's this about a dig?"

Nancy told her, whereupon Bess cried out, "You mean you might have to help dig up skeletons?"

"Oh, I don't think so," Nancy replied, "but that's what these students are doing. We'd just board at the farmhouse."

"We?" Bess asked.

"You and George and I."

"When are you going?" Bess asked.

"Tomorrow, maybe."

Bess said this would be impossible for her and George. "I guess you forgot that our cousin, Marian Shaw, is being married next week and we're to be bridesmaids."

"Of course," said Nancy.

"But," Bess went on, "if you don't find out the secret of the hollow oak right away, maybe George and I could join you later."

Nancy knew there was no use in asking her father to change his mind, so she said nothing. Both he and Hannah noticed how downcast she was.

The following morning as Mr. Drew was about to leave for his office, he said, "I'm sorry, but I feel you shouldn't be out there alone. Suppose Miss Bancroft has no room for you!"

Nancy nodded and kissed him good-by. After he had left and she had helped Hannah tidy the kitchen, the telephone rang.

She hurried to answer it and the next moment was saying, "Ned! It's so good to hear from you!"

Ned Nickerson was a good-looking, dark-haired college student on the Emerson football team. Nancy frequently shared her mystery adventures with him.

"I called you night before last but found you'd gone to New York. Just having fun or are you on a new case?" he teased.

Nancy told him the whole story, concluding with her great disappointment at not being able to go to Illinois.

There was a moment of silence, then Ned said, "Hold everything! I just had a brainstorm. A cousin of mine at Paulson is about to join the Theresa Bancroft dig. She's a swell gal. Want me to try to get in touch with her? You two might work something out. Her name's Carswell—Julie Anne Carswell."

Nancy's heart leaped. "I'm sure Dad would agree to that."

Ned said he would contact his cousin at once and get the full story about the dig and whether there would be room for Nancy at the farmhouse. Late that afternoon when Mr. Drew gave her permission to go with Julie Anne, Nancy's spirits soared.

Two days went by before Julie Anne phoned Nancy. After introducing herself, she said, "I think it's wonderful about your coming out to the dig. There's plenty of room in the farmhouse. I'll try to get in touch with Theresa—we all call her that at school—but if I can't, it's perfectly all right for you to come along with me."

"Oh, Julie Anne, you're wonderful!" Nancy exclaimed, hardly daring to believe her good fortune.

Julie Anne suggested that the two girls meet at the Riverside Hotel in St. Louis the following day. "I can't wait to see you," she added. Nancy gave a happy chuckle. "You and I have the same thought!"

The following morning Bess and George drove Nancy to an out-of-town airport where she could catch a plane that went directly to St. Louis. George parked the car and the girls hurried into the terminal building. Bess handed Nancy a package.

Nancy looked surprised. Bess smiled and said, "Some cookies I baked for you last night. I hope you don't mind carrying them."

"Of course not," Nancy replied. "Thanks. You're a dear."

She quickly fitted the box into her suitcase. Then she checked in at the ticket counter and her luggage was whisked away.

"I certainly wish you girls were going," Nancy said. "Don't forget your promise. If I haven't solved the mystery by the time the wedding is over, you *will* come?"

"We'll be there," George said.

Nancy kissed the two girls and went off to board her plane. Always alert to what was going on around her, she had had a feeling for the past ten minutes that a man was watching her rather closely. Now he got into line directly behind her. Nancy instinctively clutched her purse closer, in case he planned to snatch it.

As she boarded the plane, the young detective

laughed at her own fears. But a moment later when she took a seat by a window, she was disturbed that the man sat down alongside her. He started talking to her.

"This your first trip to St. Louis?" he asked.

"Yes," she answered truthfully, and turned her head to look out the window.

"Is someone meeting you?" the stranger went on.

"Oh yes," Nancy replied, and hoped this would end the conversation.

But the man continued to talk, asking questions about where she lived, why she was going to St. Louis, and how long she planned to be there. Nancy became evasive in her answers.

She began to wonder what ulterior motive he might have. Was he about to ask her for a date, or did he perhaps know the purpose of her mission?

By this time the plane was airborne and passengers had removed their seat belts. The stewardess came down the aisle with magazines and Nancy took one, hoping to indicate to her annoying companion she preferred reading to conversing with him. But her attempt was futile. He kept on talking, becoming more and more inquisitive as the moments passed.

The airplane was traveling at high speed and Nancy wished some unseen force would land it at once in St. Louis. Since this was not possible, she decided to get up and walk back to the galley where she could hear preparations for luncheon being started.

Nancy stood up. "Excuse me," she said, and stepped across the man's feet.

She was dangling her handbag in one hand and in her haste to leave the stranger did not notice that the strap had caught on the arm of his aisle seat.

As she moved on, the bag flew open and the contents spilled onto the floor!

Instantly her seatmate jumped up and began to help her collect the various articles. To her annoyance, he looked at each one carefully before dropping it into her handbag. A woman passenger across the aisle had also arisen and assisted Nancy in retrieving her personal belongings.

"It's a shame," the woman said, then she whispered, "You'd better get away from that man. He's a troublemaker!"

"What do you mean?" Nancy asked.

Before the woman could reply, the plane hit an air pocket. As the craft dropped, Nancy was sent sprawling in the aisle.

CHAPTER III

The Weird Voice

QUICKLY Nancy picked herself up and hurried to the galley. She told a stewardess she wanted to change her seat and was assigned one next to an elderly woman who was sleeping. Nancy leaned back and reflected on what she had heard about her former seatmate.

"So he's a troublemaker," she thought. "I can't speak right now to that woman across from him, but I must catch her at the airport and ask what she meant."

A new concern came into Nancy's mind. The man could have seen the entire contents of her handbag. He might use the information of her identity to her disadvantage! Her thoughts were interrupted by the stewardess ready to serve a luncheon tray.

The woman alongside Nancy awakened and

greeted her in a friendly way. While the two ate,
they discussed the weather and air travel in general. As soon as the woman had finished eating,
she went back to sleep and Nancy once more
thought about the annoying stranger.

"No doubt all those questions he asked me—
the snoopy old thing—were answered when he
saw the contents of my handbag."

A little while later the plane circled over the
St. Louis airport and came in for a perfect landing.

When Nancy reached the baggage-claim section
she scanned the crowd of waiting passengers, trying to spot the woman who had given her the
startling information. Unfortunately she could
not find her and finally assumed that the woman
either was carrying her own luggage or did not
have any with her.

The young detective noticed the inquisitive
stranger with whom she had sat for a while and
made a point of avoiding him. Without waiting
for a porter, she claimed her two bags and rushed
through the building to get a taxi.

"The Riverside Hotel," she told the driver.

As the taxi threaded its way through the heavy
traffic Nancy could see a high silvery arch in the
distance.

"That's our famous arch," said the driver
proudly. "It stands in a park on the bank of the

Mississippi and symbolizes that St. Louis is the Gateway to the West. The hotel you're staying at has a good view of it," he added.

When they arrived, a tall pretty girl with ginger-colored hair met Nancy in the lobby. "Hi!" she said, smiling. "I'm Julie Anne Carswell. I recognize you from a picture Ned once showed me."

Nancy laughed. "He never told me. Julie Anne, it's great to meet you."

"Actually," said Julie Anne, "I feel as if I know you and George and Bess and your friends Burt and Dave from Ned's descriptions."

"The girls might come out here to help me solve the mystery, Julie Anne. They're wonderful. You'll love them."

The two travelers registered and were assigned to a room on the fifth floor.

While Nancy changed her shoes, she said, "Now tell me about the dig."

"They're making good progress," Julie Anne replied. "Our leader, Theresa Bancroft, keeps everyone busy. They've already unearthed a skeleton of the ancient Hopewell Indians who buried their dead in great earthen mounds. No one knows what these Indians called themselves. Their first mound to be excavated was on the Hopewell farm in Ohio, so the Indians have been named that. Maybe you'll be able to find a skeleton, Nancy."

"Sounds interesting," Nancy said, "but actually

I'm here to solve a mystery about a hollow oak."

Julie Anne said that Ned had mentioned it on the phone but had given no details. "Is the case a secret?"

"Oh no," Nancy told her, and gave a brief summary about the Canadian missionary and the legend that he had left a valuable message in a hollow oak tree.

"You don't have much to go on, do you?" Julie Anne asked.

"Only one clue. A friend of my aunt's in New York found a fallen tree on which there was a plate bearing Père François's initials and an arrow. It is thought that the arrow indicated the next place the missionary was going."

"So you'll be trying to trace his journey," Julie Anne remarked, "until you find the message."

Just then the telephone rang. Nancy picked up the receiver. A man's voice on the other end said, "Nancy Drew?"

"Yes."

"This is Room 412. I have something of yours you dropped on the plane. May I come up and give it to you?"

By this time Nancy had recognized the voice of the annoying passenger. She said to him, "My friend and I will meet you in the lobby."

"Okay, if that's the way you want it. Can you come right down?"

"Yes."

Nancy turned to Julie Anne and told her what had happened on the plane and that now the man wanted to return something to her. "Come on, let's go!"

Julie Anne picked up the room key and slipped it into her purse. Then the two girls went down to the lobby. The man from the plane walked over quickly toward Nancy and said, "I have a surprise for you."

The stranger did not identify himself by name and Nancy did not introduce Julie Anne. The three went to a group of chairs and sat down.

Smiling, the man said to Nancy, "You know, you're a little fox. I thought you were coming back to your seat and have lunch with me. It was not until after you had left the plane that I found this."

He reached into a coat pocket and pulled out a small picture of Mr. Drew. With a smirk, the man asked, "Boy friend? Isn't he a little old for you?"

Nancy was disgusted with the stranger's crude humor. The picture was one of her father. She reached to get it.

"Thank you very much," she said. "I appreciate your taking the trouble to return it."

She and Julie Anne arose and started off. "What's the hurry?" the man asked.

Nancy did not reply. She merely thanked him again and the two girls walked away. He followed them a short distance, saying, "I'll be seeing you."

Julie Anne turned toward him. "What do you mean?"

At this the stranger merely laughed and walked off.

When he was out of earshot, Julie Anne remarked, "Nancy, I'm glad that man didn't insist upon a date to give you the picture. I think he's horrible."

As soon as the annoying stranger had disappeared, Julie Anne suggested that the two girls take a trip around the city. As they were about to leave the lobby, Nancy suddenly saw the woman who had warned her on the plane.

"There's someone I must talk to," she told Julie Anne and rushed across the lobby. "Hello," she said pleasantly.

The woman smiled and Nancy went on, "I wanted so much to ask you about that man who was my seatmate on the plane. I was afraid I might not see you again."

"I'm glad we met," the woman replied, and said she was Mrs. Waters. Nancy told her who she was and introduced Julie Anne who had followed her.

Mrs. Waters said the man's name was Kadle. Nancy showed her surprise and Mrs. Waters asked, "You've heard of him?"

"Not until recently," Nancy said. "A friend in New York told me to be wary of him, just as you did."

Mrs. Walters said that she believed Kit Kadle was a confidence man. "A brother-in-law of mine was one of his victims." Mrs. Waters went on, "Kadle doesn't know me, but my brother-in-law showed me pictures of him. He probably was working one of his con games on the friend you speak of in New York. He may have been planning to get you to sign up for some scheme or to take your money for a phony investment."

Nancy laughed. "No chance of that," she said, "but I appreciate your telling me all this and I'll certainly keep my eyes open for Mr. Kit Kadle."

After a few minutes of conversation the girls said good-by and went out to start their sightseeing trip. Julie Anne was a little worried about Kit Kadle, but Nancy begged her to forget him. "Let's see St. Louis."

"One of the most colorful sections of town is right here at the waterfront," Julie Anne said. "We can ride a little old-fashioned trolley car. It will take us to a number of interesting places including the arch and the old-time paddle wheel steamers at the foot of the levee."

"That sounds like fun," Nancy said eagerly. "Let's try the arch first."

At the next corner the girls boarded a yellow streetcar which clanged its bell and rode off slowly and smoothly toward the huge arch in the waterfront park. They got out with several other tourists and followed them across a concrete walk.

Then they went down a ramp toward the entrance into one leg of the huge span.

Julie Anne was a little ahead of Nancy and found herself separated from her companion by the other visitors. Suddenly the tall girl stopped short in amazement. Through the glass doors leading into the arch she saw Nancy coming toward her!

"But that's impossible," Julie Anne told herself. "How could Nancy have gotten into the arch before me and now be coming out?"

But there was no mistaking that figure! It was Nancy approaching her on the other side of the glass doors. "Nancy!" Julie Anne called and hurried forward.

Nancy laughed. "Here I am!" she answered. But her voice was coming from behind Julie Anne! "I'm in back of you!"

Julie Anne turned. There was Nancy hurrying down the ramp. "It's my reflection you saw," she said.

The other girl grinned. As they reached the doors into the arch, she saw that the darkish glass had perfectly reflected the walk behind her, making it look as if Nancy were already inside the building.

"You fooled me that time," Julie Anne said with a chuckle. "But no more trick mirrors, please!"

The girls took a slow but thrilling ride to the

top of the arch in a small, globe-shaped elevator. From there they had a breathtaking view of Illinois across the river. When they came down, the girls walked to the levee and visited a museum on an old paddle wheel steamer.

"Those river boats saw lots of good times, I guess," Nancy remarked.

Afterward, the two ate dinner in a river steamer anchored nearby. It was furnished elegantly in nineteenth-century style.

"Um! It's delicious," said Julie Anne, biting into a broiled, freshly caught fish topped with buttered almonds. Over dessert Julie Anne told Nancy that she had engaged a helicopter pilot to take the two girls south the following morning directly to the dig. The hotel would pack a lunch.

They were up early and set off for the airport. When the craft had been airborne about an hour, Nancy became fascinated by the unusual river country landscape. It was like a wide peninsula with a river on each side. To their right lay the wide brown Mississippi and ahead on the left they could see the bluish water of the Ohio.

Here and there the pilot pointed out sites of Indian burial mounds. "Many others have been leveled off and the ground used for farming," he explained.

The dig that the girls were heading for was near the Ohio River. After lunch the copter landed beyond an old-fashioned farmhouse. Near it, digging in an ancient Indian burial ground was being carried on.

Julie Anne's college friends had heard the whirlybird coming and left their work to greet the newcomers. They were so warm and friendly that Nancy's instant reaction was, "What a wonderful bunch of people!"

Bringing up the rear was a tall, blond, attractive woman who looked very trim in her pale-blue dungarees. Julie Anne introduced her as Theresa Bancroft, the group's leader.

"I'm delighted to meet you," Theresa said. "Welcome to our humble quarters."

Nancy replied, smiling, "It's kind of you to let me stay here while I try solving a mystery."

Theresa put an arm through Nancy's and led her to the farmhouse. The others followed and it seemed as if everyone was talking at once.

Several told about the perfect skeleton they had unearthed that day. While some of the girls were cooking supper, the boys in the group began singing. Soon everyone joined in.

By the time the meal was over, Nancy felt well acquainted with all the diggers from Paulson University. One of the boys, Art Budlow, who was slender, thin-faced, and had brown hair, asked the young detective if she would tell them about her mystery.

Nancy smiled. "I'm trying to find a certain oak

tree which was already hollow in 1680," she replied.

There were exclamations of surprise, and a boy named Todd Smith shook his head, saying, "You'll never do it."

Julie Anne came to Nancy's defense. "There's no harm in trying," she remarked. "Anyway, I expect Nancy to find something important right here in this dig."

Nancy laughed and said she hoped she would not disappoint anyone.

"You won't," Julie Anne assured her.

Presently the boys said good night and went off to their own quarters at another farmhouse. Nancy was placed with five girls who shared a dormitory-type bedroom.

The only bureau in it stood next to her cot, and was already filled with the other girls' clothes, so she did not unpack hers. But she opened her suitcase to take out Bess's cookies which she passed around to her roommates. They set the leftovers in the box on top of the bureau.

Nancy undressed hurriedly and crawled into bed. She fell asleep instantly, but soon afterward was aroused by a weird voice calling, "Na-an-cy Dr-ew!"

Before she could force herself wide awake, something hit her on the head.

CHAPTER IV

Rough Ride

THE object which had struck Nancy was not heavy and had not injured her. But the sensation awakened her fully. She looked straight ahead and blinked in disbelief. Two eyes were shining in the darkness. An animal!

Quickly Nancy felt under her pillow and pulled out a flashlight, which she always kept within reach when camping. She beamed it directly on the two eyes.

"Na-a-a! Na-a-a!"

A goat! It had been after the cookies and had knocked the box off the bureau. By this time all the girls were awake and flashlights shone from every cot.

"Oh!" Julie Anne cried out. "How did he get in here?"

One of the girls, Susan Miller, lighted a lantern and the whole group began to giggle. Then they asked one another how the goat had managed to enter the house. Though the front and rear doors of the farmhouse had been closed, they were not locked.

"And our bedroom door is open," added Julie Anne. "My guess is that some of the boys played a joke on us."

Nancy spoke up. "If so, I guess it was meant for me, because just before the box of cookies fell on my head, someone called through the window here, "Na-an-cy Dr-ew!"

By this time she was trying to lead the goat from the room. Apparently remembering the cookies, he was reluctant to go.

Nancy took a couple of them from the box and enticed the animal out of the house. She threw the cookies on the ground, gave him a gentle shove, then shut and locked the front door. Julie Anne had followed her and now decided to lock the rear door also.

"It must have been the boys' doings," she said. "Who else would bother to come way out here to play a joke?"

Nancy agreed. The girls returned to their cots and all the lights were turned off. Fortunately the disturbance had not awakened others who were in the house.

In the morning the boys arrived early, and Theresa held a short Sunday religious service before breakfast. As they ate, the boys were questioned about having played a joke on Nancy and the other girls the night before. All of them looked blank and denied having had any part in it.

Julie Anne did not believe them and tried to get them to admit their guilt. The boys, however, insisted they knew nothing about the trick.

Nancy had begun to believe them, and this brought a new worry to her mind. Was it possible that Kit Kadle had followed up his announcement that she and Julie Anne would be seeing him? It seemed to Nancy a logical conclusion.

If the man was determined to find the hollow oak with the message in it, and had learned she had solved many mysteries, it was highly possible he was nearby to spy on her. He would try to intimidate her into leaving the area. She said nothing about it to Julie Anne or the others.

While Nancy was still speculating about Kadle, a farm truck came rattling into the yard. Everyone rushed outside.

A tall, slender, slightly-stooped man stepped to the ground. The goat, which had been munching grass and herbs, walked over to him.

"The man must be his owner," Nancy thought as the stranger came forward.

"Howdy, folks. Good mornin'. I see you got my goat."

Several of the girls giggled. Art called out, "Did we?"

The farmer paid no attention to Art's pun. He

said, "I'm Clem Rucker and I live a piece away
from here. Somebody opened my goat pen last
night and took out Sammy Boy. Did one o' you
fellows do it?"

The boys shook their heads. Nancy now explained what little she knew about the episode.
Clem shrugged. "Some mysteries just ain't goin'
to be solved."

His remark gave Nancy an idea. "Mr. Rucker,
maybe you—"

"Oh, call me Clem," the farmer said. "I ain't
used to this mister stuff."

Nancy grinned. "All right. I have a map showing where there's a certain oak tree I'd like to see.
Will you wait a moment while I get the map?"

She hurried into the farmhouse and was back
in a couple of minutes. Nancy unfolded the sketch
which the New York detective had made and
showed it to Clem. He smiled.

"I know all about this," he said. "You're lookin'
for the secret message in the oak tree, same as
them city detectives who were up here on their
vacation. Sure," he added, "be glad to take you
around. That is, if you don't mind ridin' in an
old car."

"I don't mind," Nancy replied. "Of course I'll
pay you for the trip."

The two arranged a price and then Nancy
turned to Julie Anne. "Could you get permission
to go with me?"

"I think so. Wait until I ask Theresa."

While she was asking, Nancy inquired when Clem could pick them up.

He gave a wide grin. "Soon as I get Sammy Boy home, I'll bring my car over and away we'll go."

Nancy was delighted that she could start work at once on the hollow oak mystery. She was glad, too, when Julie Anne received permission to accompany her.

Sammy Boy was lifted into the farm truck and Clem drove off. An hour later the old man was back.

Nancy and Julie Anne found it hard to keep from laughing aloud at the conveyance which was to take them on their detective trip. The car was a very old four-passenger type with no top and had rather narrow wheels.

Nancy thought, "This should be on exhibit in an antique car museum!"

The two girls climbed into the back seat and Clem drove off. The old car was amazing. Though the cushions were worn thin and the girls bounced up and down on the rough road, the engine purred along satisfactorily. Clem was a fast driver and did not seem to mind the bumpiness of the ride.

A few minutes later he turned off the road suddenly and started across a plowed field. The girls held on tightly. Clem pointed to his left.

"See that little higher section with corn growin'

on it? That was once a dig and they found plenty o' old Indian bones there."

"It certainly doesn't look like much now," Julie Anne remarked.

"That's right," said Clem. "Folks is funny. They make such a to-do about takin' care o' cemeteries but they sure ain't got no respect for the skeletons o' folks that lived around here three or four hundred years ago."

Nancy made no comment. She was deep in thought, recalling how carefully the Egyptians of thousands of years ago preserved their mummies.

Her reflections were interrupted when Clem made a sharp right turn and drove up a slightly hilly section.

"Was this an Indian gravesite?" Julie Anne asked.

"I don't know," Clem replied. "So far as I've heard, nobody has ever come to dig it up."

When he reached the top of the incline which had not been cultivated and was covered with coarse grass, he stopped abruptly.

"Here's the stump o' that oak you're lookin' for, Nancy," he said.

Both girls hopped out of the car and went over to the stump. Nancy turned to Clem. "Where is the tree trunk?"

He pointed down the slope. Among some bushes lay a giant tree. Nancy hurried down to it.

Facing her was a small lead plate embedded in the trunk. On the plate had been etched *Père François 1675*. Underneath the inscription was an arrow.

The trunk was hollow but the outer part was still in good condition. The tree that had stood at the top of the slope more than three hundred years ago apparently had been blown over recently.

Nancy remarked, "I understand that when the tree was standing, the arrow pointed east."

Clem chuckled. "Now I just might be able to help you figure out that one."

The girls watched him as he walked along the side of the tree, then climbed back to the stump. After two such trips he said, "I reckon from the pattern o' that stump and the bottom o' this tree that they fitted together so the arrow pointed due east."

"Can you drive us in that direction?" Nancy asked.

"You never get anywhere if you don't try," Clem answered with a chuckle.

They all climbed into his old car and he set off. Clem continued to drive through farms and woods. Once they forded a stream. But he avoided taking any of the roads, although they had crossed several of them.

"Roads ain't much better'n the fields," he explained with a grin. "Besides, they wind around too much. We can go quicker this way. I'm aimin' for a nice picnic spot."

"That's good," said Julie Anne. "I'm starved."

Five minutes later Clem stopped near a stream and they all got out. Julie Anne and Nancy had packed enough lunch for all of them. Clem also started to open a package of food.

"My wife Hortense," he said, "makes the best beaten biscuits you ever ate. Then she opens 'em and puts a little fishball inside. I brought along some of 'em."

The girls found the stuffed beaten biscuits delicious and said so. "Please tell your wife they're great," Nancy added, "and thanks to you both for supplying part of the lunch."

While they ate, Clem told one exaggerated story after another and kept the girls laughing all the time.

"One more and then we got to go," he said. "Once there was an Indian fishin' in the Ohio River. That ain't a long way from here, you know. He was standin' in the water with a club in his hand gettin' ready to whack a fish when it swam past. Well, a fish come along all right, but before the Indian had a chance to whack it, the thing jumped right out o' the water and knocked him over."

"What a whopper!" Julie Anne exclaimed.

"Now that ain't so much of a whopper as you

might think," Clem replied. "We used to have catfish in the Ohio River as big as seals."

Clem said there were no more big fish in the river, then abruptly changed the subject. "Would you like to see my good-luck coin?"

He drew a coin from his pocket the size of a half dollar and handed it to Nancy. The wording on the coin was so worn that she could not make it out and reached into a pocket of her jeans for a magnifying glass. Nancy held it over the coin.

A moment later she asked excitedly, "Clem, do you know what it says on here?"

CHAPTER V

Air Spy

JULIE Anne and Clem listened in fascination while Nancy translated what was engraved on the coin. It was in French. At the top were the initials P. F. and underneath a short prayer.

"Père François!" exclaimed Julie Anne.

"I'm sure it is," said Nancy. "He must have dropped it in this area or else the Indians took it away from him and lost it themselves."

There was no date on the metal disk but the girls assumed it was over three hundred years old.

"This isn't exactly a good-luck piece," Nancy stated. "It's much more."

Clem looked at her intently. "Whatever it is, it don't mean nothin' to me. I bought it from the lad who found it. I'm givin' it to you, Nancy."

"May I pay you something for it?" she asked.

Clem Rucker laughed. "What would I do with

a lot o' money? I only gave that lad twenty-five cents, so I'm not out much."

"Well, this is a fabulous gift," Nancy said, "and I shall treasure it."

"Anyway," said Clem, standing up, "I hope it brings you good luck in solvin' the mystery o' the hollow oak. We'd better go on."

He followed a course due east and in about half an hour they came to another hollow oak. This one was still standing and from its size they judged it was centuries old. Clem said he thought the tree might have been there as long as four hundred years.

Nancy walked around the oak and found a rotted-out section. She beamed her flashlight inside and put her face to the edge of the hole to see what was in the cavity. Unfortunately she found nothing.

No marker was showing but there was definitely a hump at one place in the bark. Clem produced a chisel from his car. He and Nancy took turns chipping and peeling off bark until they uncovered part of a lead plate.

A short time later the three searchers became aware of a helicopter circling overhead. As they glanced up, Nancy detected someone with binoculars looking at them.

"He's spying on us!"

The copter suddenly flew off and disappeared. But not before Nancy had opened her purse and written down the license number on a pad. She suspected that Kit Kadle might be a passenger in the helicopter and she meant to find out.

"Have you ever seen that copter before?" Nancy asked Clem.

"Oh yes," the farmer replied. "Guess he's one o' them free-lance pilots. Takes folks up to give 'em a bird's-eye view of the burial mounds and the river."

Meanwhile Julie Anne, who had taken the chisel from Clem, had chipped off more of the bark. Suddenly she exclaimed, "Here's another Père François plate! There's no date on this one and only the initials P. F., but I can see a faint arrow. This one points directly south."

"It may lead to what was once an Indian settlement," Nancy mused. "We know Père François traveled from village to village trying to convert the Indians."

"Could be," said the farmer, "but I don't reckon we can find out today. I'm sorry, ladies, but I have to get home now and tend to my chores."

"When can you help us again?" Nancy asked him.

Clem said he would not be able to for another three days and he did not know of anyone else who might take Nancy around on her search.

"Anyway," said Julie Anne, "I won't be able to leave the dig."

"He's spying on us!" Nancy exclaimed

Nancy was disappointed over the delay. But in the meantime she would try to find out about the helicopter pilot and who his passenger was.

Clem took a shortcut back to the dig. The girls thanked him for the trip and said they would expect him in three days.

As Clem drove away, Nancy thought, "I'll have to figure a way to get to town so I can find out about that copter."

It was nearly suppertime and the diggers had stopped work. Nancy and Julie Anne found the other girls preparing a wholesome meal. Meanwhile, the boys were cleaning the artifacts and fossils which they had discovered at the bottom of a new pit.

All of them were eager to hear what progress Nancy had made on her case. She related the details, including Clem's story about the catfish. The others laughed and Art burst into a song from the opera *Porgy and Bess* about Catfish Row.

When he finished, Nancy announced, "I'd like to drive some place to make a phone call. I forgot to ask Clem if he has a telephone."

Art spoke up. "I have a two-seater motorcycle here," he told her. "I'll be glad to take you to town."

"That's wonderful," Nancy said. "Could we go tomorrow morning?"

"You bet," he said. "But it will have to be early. My shift begins at ten A.M."

"Where do you think the pilot came from?" Nancy asked him.

Art said there was a small airfield outside the town of Walmsley, the nearest one to the dig.

They had a very early breakfast and left the dig site at seven o'clock. Art drove directly to Walmsley and went on to the airfield which was about three miles out of town.

When they arrived Nancy stepped into the office and asked who owned the helicopter with the license number she had copied on her pad. She showed it to the man in charge.

"Oh, that's Roscoe Thompson," he replied.

"Is he around now? I'd like to speak to him," Nancy said.

Thompson was at the end of the field checking his helicopter. Nancy and Art walked over to him.

Roscoe proved to be a very pleasant young man and gladly answered Nancy's questions. His passenger the day before had been a man named Tom Wilson.

"Where does he come from?" Nancy questioned.

"I really don't know. He didn't talk much. Said he wanted to make the trip over the site of the various Indian burial mounds. Mr. Wilson was interested to learn their locations because he's an amateur archaeologist.

"By the way," Roscoe went on, "Mr. Wilson was very curious about two girls and a man who were hacking at an oak tree. Was one of them you?"

"Yes," Nancy admitted. "Why did your passenger want to know what I was doing?"

"He didn't say."

Roscoe asked Nancy if she would like to speak to Tom Wilson. When she said Yes, the pilot told her he expected the man to arrive at the airfield about midmorning.

"I'll introduce you," he said.

This was just what Nancy wanted! She turned to Art, "Could you possibly stay a little longer?"

The archaeology student shook his head. "Sorry, but a promise is a promise. I must be back at the dig by ten. Several of us are working on a certain section and each one of us has a particular task."

"I understand," Nancy said.

Seeing Nancy's look of disappointment, Art said, "Maybe this Tom Wilson will get here before ten. I can give you a half hour. In the meantime I'll run into town and pick up some food supplies."

Nancy was grateful. "I'll make a few phone calls. If Mr. Wilson should arrive, will you let me know?" she asked Roscoe.

"Will do."

The young detective hurried to a phone booth alongside the airfield building. She called her home, hoping her father would still be there, but he had already left for his law office.

Hannah Gruen reported that everything was fine, and Bess and George were eager to join Nancy. "They still want to help you solve the mystery—that is, unless you have already done so."

"I'm far from solving it," Nancy answered. "The case is fascinating, but I'm making very slow progress. By the way, you can write or telegraph me in care of Clem Rucker at Walmsley. He'll bring the message over to the dig."

Nancy had just said this when there was a tap on the glass door of the booth. She turned to see Roscoe standing there.

As Nancy pushed open the door a crack, the pilot said, "Here comes Mr. Wilson now!"

CHAPTER VI

Ear to the Ground

"OH, Hannah, I must go now," Nancy said hurriedly. "I'll call again."

She hung up the phone and rushed from the booth. Roscoe motioned her to follow him. A short distance ahead a gray-haired man with a decided limp was approaching the building. He had a full mustache and a chin beard.

"This can't be Kit Kadle," Nancy told herself, and yet there seemed to be something familiar about the man. Roscoe introduced him and Nancy.

"Pleased to meet you," Mr. Wilson said in an affected voice.

Nancy found herself staring intently at him. Could he be Kit Kadle in disguise?

Mr. Wilson smiled. "Aren't you the girl I saw hacking at a tree near a dig site?"

"Yes I am," Nancy replied.

When she gave no explanation, he asked her why she was doing it. Nancy smiled and replied, "Just examining the oak." She changed the subject. "Weren't you staying at the Riverside Hotel in St. Louis?"

The man shook his head. "Never heard of it," he said in his affected voice and limped off. Nancy wondered where he was going.

At that moment Art roared up on his motorcycle. Nancy climbed aboard and they headed for the dig. Art asked her if she had learned anything.

"Yes and no," she replied. "I talked with Mr. Wilson. I think he's Kit Kadle in disguise."

"Whether he's Kit Kadle or Tom Wilson," said Art, "I advise you to forget him."

"Okay," Nancy agreed. "At least I won't talk about him."

"Don't get the wrong idea," Art said. "I want to see you solve the mystery and I'd like to help but right now let's just enjoy this ride!"

Nancy made a point of doing just that. She and Art laughed and joked the rest of the way to the dig. They found everyone else at work. The only person not in or around the pit was Julie Anne, whose turn it was to prepare luncheon. She was in the kitchen struggling with an old-fashioned oil-burning stove.

"This oven just won't get hot," she complained. "I'm afraid to turn the burners any higher for fear I might blow up the whole house!"

As Nancy helped her adjust the stove, she told Julie Anne about Mr. Wilson. Then, after changing her clothes, she went to the barn which was being used as a laboratory.

Several students were seated at trestle tables brushing dirt from bones and bits of pottery. One girl was patiently putting together pieces of a broken bowl.

"What can I do to help?" Nancy asked Theresa.

"Dig," she answered with a smile. Theresa handed Nancy a child-sized shovel, a teaspoon, a fine sieve, and a camel's-hair dusting brush.

"Every inch of ground is important," the leader said. "You must work very carefully in order not to discard anything worth saving."

Nancy promised to be cautious and walked over to the excavation in front of the farmhouse. It seemed much larger than when she had first arrived. Nevertheless she scrambled down the side, thinking, "If they go much deeper, the diggers will need a ladder."

After watching the other workers for several minutes, Nancy knelt and gently used the little shovel to place earth in the sieve. Carefully she crumbled it through the fine wire mesh. All that remained in the strainer were several pieces of gravel. After four tries she had about decided there was nothing in that spot, when a tiny piece of white caught her eye. She moved closer to it and this time used her teaspoon. Suddenly she had a chunk of earth on it which contained a piece of bone. Excitedly Nancy put it into the sieve and gently shook the dirt. In a few moments a bone fragment half an inch long lay exposed.

Gleefully Nancy cried out, "I've found something!"

The other diggers hurried to her side.

"Do you think it's a finger bone?" asked Julie Anne, who had joined the group.

At once Claire Warwick spoke up. "That's obviously a metatarsal bone, not a phalange."

"Not a what?" asked Nancy.

"Phalange—that's what we scientists call toe or finger bones," Claire replied loftily. "But this is neither one. It's part of the skeleton of the forefoot."

"Wait a minute," said Theresa, stepping forward. "Let's see that."

Nancy handed her the bit of bone.

"This is a segment of an infant's finger," said Theresa. "Better check your anatomy book again, Claire."

Two boys, with whom Claire was not popular, burst into laughter. "Better watch out, Claire," said Bill Munson. "First thing you know you'll be connecting the ankle bones to the neck bones."

The girl flushed angrily, but said nothing.

Theresa urged Nancy to look for more of the skeleton and she worked diligently the rest of the day, but had no luck.

Finally it was quitting time. The weary diggers came to the surface, and went to change their clothes. Some started to prepare supper.

Nancy came outside and dropped to the ground for a brief rest and to think about the secret in the hollow oak. She found herself dozing and turned on her side.

Suddenly her attention was directed to a sound she detected on the ground. Listening closely, Nancy decided it was a car. Who was coming?

She sat up and watched the road that led to the dig. No car appeared, so again the young detective put her ear to the ground and listened. Now there was nothing but silence.

"Someone must have parked," she thought.

The idea made her uneasy. She stood up and went into the house. A few of the boys had gathered in the living room. Nancy told them what she had heard.

"Maybe I'm silly to be suspicious," she said, "but I have a hunch that Kit Kadle may come here and attempt some mischief. You know, two people have warned me against him."

Art spoke up. "I don't think you're silly at all. This house and the dig should be protected as well as you. Okay with you guys if we take turns standing guard here at night?"

"Great idea," replied Bob Snell. "You give out the shifts and I'll be on the job."

Nancy smiled at them all. "I'm sorry to be a troublemaker in your group, but—"

"Stop that!" Art interrupted her. "It will be an exciting change to play detective." He arranged time shifts and took the first one himself.

Dinner was announced. The group ate heartily and retired early. Nancy found it hard to sleep. She could not keep her mind off the fact that Kit Kadle might show up at the farmhouse. If so, what would he try to do? She felt sure he was the one who had let the goat into the house. This time his mischief might cause serious harm.

Finally, after tossing and turning for an hour, she got up, pulled on her clothes, and went outdoors. It was a bright, starry night and objects were clearly distinguishable.

Almost instantly Art was at her side. He gave a low chuckle. "I thought you were Kit Kadle's girl friend."

Nancy grinned and started to walk around the farmhouse with him. Just then they became aware of light footsteps not far away. The couple hid behind bushes.

The stealthy footsteps came from the rear of the house. Nancy and Art fully expected someone to enter the front door. Instead they saw a man going toward the dig carrying a ladder.

Moving quietly the couple followed him across

the yard and into the field. They saw the figure set the ladder into the excavation.

Nancy whispered. "It's time to act!"

She and Art loped with light steps toward the dig. The man heard them and turned quickly. Nancy recognized him. Art beamed his flashlight on the figure.

"Tom Wilson!" Nancy whispered.

They ran toward the man to question him about why he had come there. But before they could reach him, Wilson took off like a frightened deer.

"He's not limping!" Nancy observed as she and Art pursued the fleeing figure. "We mustn't lose him!" she exclaimed.

Wilson was fleet-footed. He had gone straight up the road, but to the young people's amazement had outdistanced them. When they lost sight of him, Nancy stopped and put her ear to the ground.

"He's still on the road," she reported, catching up to Art.

A few seconds later Nancy listened again. They were closer now! She and Art put on extra speed.

"We're catching up!" she gasped.

They raced along the road like marathon runners.

CHAPTER VII

River Pirates

WHILE Nancy and Art were running after the fleeting figure, Todd Smith came to the farmhouse to relieve Art. He looked all around for his friend and finally decided he had better report his absence to Theresa Bancroft.

As he reached the door, Julie Anne rushed out. She almost bumped into him.

"Nancy's not in her bed!" she exclaimed.

Todd looked puzzled. "I was just coming to report that Art's missing. I'm sure he wouldn't have left the farmhouse unguarded. Something strange must have happened, Julie Anne!"

"They're probably together," she said. "I hope they're not in danger! Let's look for them."

Both Julie Anne and Todd had flashlights. They began walking around the grounds and finally came to the dig.

"Look!" Julie Anne exclaimed. "Someone put a ladder into the pit."

The two flashlights did not reveal anyone in the excavation. The searchers were more puzzled than ever.

"What could have happened?" Julie Anne asked.

"Listen! I hear people talking," Todd said.

They moved toward the sound and in a few minutes saw two flashlights bobbing. Their own lights revealed Nancy and Art.

"What's going on?" Todd demanded.

"Did you see the ladder?" Art queried.

"Yes. Whose is it?"

Nancy and Art related what they had seen and their chase after Tom Wilson. "We had almost caught up to him when he jumped into a car and rode off," Nancy explained.

"But I thought Tom Wilson was lame," Julie Anne remarked.

"So did I," Nancy replied. "That man's a fake and I'm sure now he's Kit Kadle in disguise."

Todd wondered what the intruder had planned to take out of the dig. No one could hazard a guess, since all the artifacts and fossils uncovered so far had been brought to the laboratory.

"Have you any idea, Nancy?" Todd asked. She shook her head.

By this time Art had pulled the ladder from the excavation. It was crudely made of narrow tree branches from an oak.

Nancy suggested that the whole affair should be

reported to the State Police in the morning, and offered to do it for Theresa. She asked Art if he would take her into town directly after breakfast to phone headquarters.

"Glad to," he replied. "Good night."

Nancy and Julie Anne went back to bed and slept soundly until Theresa rang the rising bell. When the other diggers learned about the night's adventure, they were alarmed. Theresa tried to calm their fears, but she herself was concerned. Why was her expedition being bothered?

Nancy was sure she could read the woman's thoughts. Going up to her, she said quietly, "You weren't having any trouble here until I arrived. My mystery must be the cause of it. I can't figure out how the hollow oak I'm looking for and your dig are connected but there must be some tie-in. I'm sure Kit Kadle is trying to discourage my sleuthing. It would be better if I leave. Then no one will be in danger."

Theresa put an arm around Nancy's shoulders. "You're going to stay," she said firmly. "What you say may be true, but as yet we have no proof. Besides, we like having you at the dig. I won't hear of your leaving."

Nancy thanked the leader and kissed her. "In any case, Art and I will report last night's episode to the State Police, if you wish us to."

"Yes indeed."

They rode away on the motorcycle and soon

reached Walmsley. Nancy telephoned the State Police, who promised to investigate at once. Next she called her father. "Dad, I'm so glad I reached you. How's everything?"

"Just fine, but Hannah and I miss you very much. Well, what's the report on the mystery?"

Nancy brought him up to date. Then Mr. Drew told his daughter that Ned Nickerson was very eager to get in touch with her. "I suggest you call him."

Nancy did this, trying three different places where she thought Ned might be. But he was not at any of them. Nancy sat in the phone booth another half a minute thinking of the tall, good-looking young man. Right now he was working on a summer job, selling insurance.

"I wonder," she thought, "if by any chance Ned is going to tell me he's coming out here." She hoped so!

Art came to see if she was ready, saying he must get back to the dig. The two roared off on the motorcycle. As they approached the farmhouse, they noticed that two state troopers were already there. With them was an elderly Indian.

Nancy dismounted and walked up to the group. She introduced herself. The troopers gave their names as Rankin and White, and introduced the Indian as Robert Lightfoot.

"Mr. Lightfoot is the one who built this ladder," Rankin said, pointing to the crude piece which lay on the ground beside them. "I've seen others like it at his cabin. He says a man who didn't give his name came to his place and wanted to buy the ladder."

The Indian took up the story. "He was a stranger. Told me he needed the ladder to prune his apple trees."

"This time of year?" Trooper White exclaimed. "That's crazy!"

Lightfoot smiled. "I think so too."

Nancy asked for a description of the man. Upon hearing that he was lame and gray-haired, she was sure he was the same person who had brought the ladder to the excavation. The Indian was amazed to learn this and said the buyer had not mentioned the dig.

The troopers walked off a little distance for a private conversation. Nancy took the opportunity to ask Lightfoot if he had heard the legend about Père François and the hollow oak.

"The missionary's treasure will never be found around here," Lightfoot replied.

"Treasure?" Nancy repeated.

"Maybe you think there was only a message," the Indian went on. "The message told about the treasure. Père François was captured by the Iroquois but he escaped. He started for the Ohio River but never got there. River pirates stole the treasure he was carrying. I am sorry to say they killed him."

"Did the legend tell what happened to the treasure?" Nancy asked.

Lightfoot nodded. "The pirates took it to the river and hid it somewhere. I think maybe in a cave. Nature punished the pirates for their thievery. A great storm overtook them and all were drowned."

Nancy was intrigued by the story. "Then the treasure might still be hidden in the cave?"

"It could be," the Indian answered.

The two troopers came over and said they must leave. They promised to start tracking down Tom Wilson. Lightfoot left with them.

As Nancy went for her digging tools, she kept thinking about the message in the hollow oak, the legendary treasure and its hiding place. Was it possible the pirates' loot could still be there?

"I'd like to hunt for it," she said to herself.

But her thoughts were interrupted when she unearthed a tiny bone. A little later she was delighted to come upon another which matched it. Theresa was thrilled.

It was not until evening that Nancy had a chance to tell Theresa about the Indian's story. The archaeologist was interested. She remarked that it was possible to go up and down the Ohio River by towboat and barge.

"While you're here, perhaps you'd like to arrange for a trip," she suggested. "You get on at Cairo."

"I'd love to," Nancy said. "Tomorrow Clem is coming to take Julie Anne and me on another search for the hollow oak with the message. If we don't find anything, perhaps it would be worth looking in caves along the river."

"The most likely one for pirates to have used would be Cave in Rock," said Theresa. "It's on the Ohio River near Elizabethtown, Illinois. For a number of years after the Revolutionary War outlaws and pirates used that cave as headquarters. From there they preyed on the flatboats carrying pioneers down the river. Now it's part of a state park."

"It sounds fascinating," said Nancy.

The next morning Clem's car rattled into the farmhouse yard. Nancy and Julie Anne were waiting with a box of lunch. Clem was cheerful as usual and full of exaggerated stories about the area. Right after he had related one about a pioneer who always shot with two guns crossed, Nancy asked him if he had ever heard of Père François and the pirates.

"Nope, can't say I have."

Nancy and Julie Anne grinned. It was fun to have a story to match Clem's! Nancy told him Lightfoot's version of the hollow oak legend.

"Well now, ain't that somethin'?" he said, removing his battered straw hat and scratching his head. "Thought I knew all the stories about this neck o' the woods."

By this time they had reached the hollow oak with the arrow pointing south and went in that direction to look for another one. After a bouncy ride they came to a stream of rushing water filled with rocks, many of them sharp.

When Clem headed for it, Julie Anne cried out, "Oh, you're not going to try crossing this?"

"I sure am," Clem replied. "Been through here many times."

The girls held on tightly as the old, open car was driven into the water. It swung from side to side and slid off the rocks. Clem had a determined look on his face.

"This is crazy!" Julie Anne whispered.

Nancy thought so too, but before she had a chance to say this out loud, the car gave a sudden jerk. The right wheels landed up on the rocks. The car tilted precariously and went out of control.

The next instant it went over on its side, throwing the occupants into the rock stream!

CHAPTER VIII

Exciting Plans

FOR a few moments after the car went over, there was no sound except that of the rushing water. Then Nancy, soaked from head to toe, arose and looked around. To her relief Julie Anne was pulling herself up. Both of them were concerned about Clem. But the next second he stood upright and gazed sheepishly at the girls.

"Sorry, ladies," he said. "I don't know what possessed this contraption. She just got stubborn. Been through here many times. But now when I have passengers, she starts to act up. You two all right?"

"Yes, I am," Nancy replied, "but soaked."

"Me too," Julie Anne added.

"I reckon you'll dry out soon, it's so hot," Clem predicted. "Want to give me a hand with this thing? We'll see if we can right her."

The old car was not heavy and though it took the combined strength of its three passengers they finally managed to set the vehicle on its four wheels. Clem climbed into the driver's seat and tried to start the motor. Dead! Its owner stepped out. As he scratched his head in perplexity, the farmer realized his hat was gone.

"Sailed on downstream, I reckon," he said with a sigh.

"And our lunch too," Julie Anne stated ruefully. "I guess we'll have to give up our sleuthing for today."

Nancy had been looking toward the shore. "Perhaps we can push the car back to the embankment, and after it dries out, the motor will start," she said hopefully.

"You may be right," Clem agreed. He heaved a sigh. "It's a long walk home and a long way to the bridge that goes across this stream. Anyhow it don't take cars. All right, let's push!"

One girl got on each side of the old car, while Clem pushed the front end and guided the steering wheel. The going was rough and the car balked at the rocks. By the time they finally reached the embankment, all of them were exhausted and flopped to the ground for a rest.

Water poured from the car. When the flow slackened, Clem opened the hood. "We'll let the sun work on this," he announced. Nevertheless he took some rags from a compartment and began sopping water from the engine.

"I predict," he said, "that this old buggy will be runnin' within half an hour."

"I certainly hope so," Julie Anne replied. She was now walking up and down letting the breeze blow through her hair and clothing.

Meanwhile Nancy had been looking around. She spotted a huge oak on the far side of the stream. Though the tree was in full leaf and looked healthy, and probably was not hollow, she wondered if there might be a lead plate on it.

"I won't be satisfied until I make certain," the young sleuth thought, and pointed out the oak to Julie Anne and Clem. "I think I'll wade over there and look."

"But you're already partially dry," Julie Anne reminded her.

She knew this would not deter Nancy and she was right. The curious young detective stepped down into the stream and made her way across. To her disappointment, she found that the tree had no lead plate on it nor any carvings or other marks.

"Well, I can't pick up a clue every time," Nancy said to herself, and recrossed the stream.

By this time Clem had dried off the motor and the many wires leading from it. Hopefully he climbed into the driver's seat and turned on the ignition. The enginer sputtered and a stream of water shot out of the exhaust. Coughing and sputtering, the motor kept going, and in three minutes purred normally.

"Yea!" Nancy and Julie Anne cried out.

The two girls got into the back seat and Clem took off. Presently Nancy asked if he knew how to go about arranging a towboat trip.

"Yep," said Clem. "I know just the fellow who can fix you up. He's an old geezer, a retired towboat captain. Lives just outside o' Cairo, about four miles up the bank o' the Ohio. You can't miss it—small white house with red trim. Name's Nathaniel Hornbeck."

"Do you have his phone number?" Nancy asked.

Clem grinned as he swerved around a hole in the dirt road. "He don't have one. You just knock on the door. He's glad for company. Sorry I disappointed you today," Clem added, "but sometime I'll come around and take you on the rest of the journey to find the hollow oak."

"Great," Nancy said. "Just let us know."

By the time they reached the dig, the trio was thoroughly dry but disheveled looking. Nancy and Julie Anne hurried into the farmhouse to change their clothes. No one was around and they assumed the diggers were busy in the excavation.

When the girls came outside, they met Theresa coming from the dig, holding something in her hand. She looked at the girls and beamed. "I've made a marvelous find!" she exclaimed.

The archaeologist opened her fingers to reveal an ancient Indian necklace of river pearls and a shell bracelet.

"These had been in a deerskin pouch," she told the girls. "Of course the pouch had disintegrated but we're saving the fragments. I'm taking these treasures to our lab."

During the rest of the day Nancy kept wondering why Ned wanted to talk to her. Since Art was not free to go into Walmsley she could not telephone, but he promised to take her the next morning.

They set off early. When they reached town, Art said he would shop while Nancy was busy. Once more she tried Ned and finally found him.

"Hi!" she said. "I'm glad I located you."

Ned Nickerson chuckled. "I was beginning to think you'd forgotten me. Have you solved the mystery?"

"No, but I have an interesting lead."

"Good. Nancy, how would you like three hearty young men and two smart girls to join you?"

Nancy almost shouted for joy. "You mean you and Burt and Dave and George and Bess can come here?"

Ned said this was exactly what he meant. "You say the word and we'll hop a plane."

"Come as soon as you can," she urged. "Fly to St. Louis and take a helicopter from there. My interesting clue is that pirates stole the treasure which Père François was carrying and hid it in a cave along the Ohio River. If the story is true, there's a good chance the treasure has never been found because all the pirates were lost in a storm."

Enthusiastically she told about the Ohio River towboat trips. "Would you and the others like to take one and hunt for the treasure?"

"Sounds great," he replied. "Suppose you make all the arrangements and then call me when you want us to start. Only don't make it too long. I'm itching to get out there."

Tingling with happiness, Nancy came out of the phone booth. Just then Art rode up. Excitedly she asked, "Would you possibly have time to dash into Cairo and back?"

He looked at his wrist watch. "Yes, if we hurry. What's up?"

Nancy swung onto the motorcycle and it roared down the road. She told Art the news that her friends were going to fly out to help solve the mystery.

When Art made no comment, she said, "You'll like them. I know you will."

He had become glum, but replied, "At any rate I'll like Bess and George."

The remark amused Nancy, but as time went

on and Art did not respond to her remarks as he usually did, she became puzzled. Then suddenly Nancy wondered, "Could Art be jealous of Ned?"

Deciding the thought was ridiculous, she put it out of her mind. It was true she and Art had been together a good deal the past few days but the friendship was casual.

As they neared Cairo after a ride with an almost one-sided conversation, Nancy decided that her hunch had been right. Art had hardly spoken the whole time. Obviously he was not thrilled by Ned's expected arrival! An idea of how to take care of the situation came to her.

"Art," she said, "do you think you and Julie Anne could get away from the dig for a few days and go on the towboat trip with the rest of us? I'd love to have you come."

Art brightened considerably. "I'm sure we could get permission. Thanks a lot."

When they reached town Nancy directed Art to Captain Hornbeck's home. In a short time they pulled up in front of a tree-shaded cottage on a low bluff overlooking the river. A tall, weather-beaten man with gray hair stood in the front doorway. In one hand he held an arrow.

"Howdy," he said, smiling. "I heard you coming on that motorcycle. What can I do for you?"

Nancy introduced herself and Art and explained what they wanted. "Clem Rucker said you have no phone, so we couldn't call you—"

"Humph!" the captain snorted. "Old Clem doesn't know. I got an unlisted number so folks won't bother me. But come in."

He led the way into a small living room crowded with furniture. On a large table Nancy and Art were amazed to see arrowheads, shafts, feathers, and odd tools.

"I make bows and arrows," the old man said, "and use the same tools as the ancient Indians."

He showed them a stone scraper he worked with to form the wooden shafts. "Then I fit a real Indian arrowhead to it," he added. "I've found hundreds of 'em around here."

While the young people admired the artifacts he had made, the retired captain called the towboat company for which he had once worked. The line was busy. When he came back, Nancy asked him about river pirates.

"In the old days," he said, "the Ohio and Mississippi both had their share of pirates. They were a menace to navigation."

Warming to the subject, Hornbeck told his callers that pirates used to lie in wait along the shore until a flatboat with a pioneer family came along. Then they would go out, capture the boat, and kill the passengers.

"How wicked!" Nancy exclaimed.

Art asked, "What did they do with the cargo?"

Captain Hornbeck said they usually took it all the way to New Orleans and sold it.

"In those days travel overland was so slow that news of a piracy did not reach New Orleans until after the men had left there."

The elderly captain went back to the telephone and tried again to get the towboat company. This time he was successful and after a short conversation arranged the trip for Nancy's group.

"You can go aboard in the evening day after tomorrow."

"That's perfect," Nancy told him. "Thank you so much. We've enjoyed talking to you."

The elderly man walked to the door with Nancy and Art. "I hope you have fun and good luck on your trip," he said.

Before returning to the dig, Nancy called the airfield. When she learned that Roscoe Thompson was not there, she left a message requesting him to pick them up Saturday morning and fly them to Cairo.

Art was more talkative and whistled cheerfully on the way back to the dig. Nancy was relieved that apparently whatever was bothering him had vanished. When they arrived at the farmhouse, Nancy thanked Art and then dashed inside to change into digging clothes. No one was around.

"I guess everyone's down in the pit," Nancy thought. "I— Oh!"

She had caught sight of a crudely printed note propped up on the bureau. Her name was scrawled across the top. Underneath was a message:

"You will never find the right hollow oak. I have taken the message out of it and destroyed the tree. Now the treasure it told about will be mine! Ha! Ha!"

CHAPTER IX

Escaping Thief

NANCY studied the note on the bureau intently. Was it true that someone had found the message in the hollow oak which told of a treasure?

The young detective took a long breath. "Maybe it's only a joke," she said to herself. "Perhaps one of the girls or even one of the boys left this note to play a trick on me."

Nancy took out her magnifying glass and examined the paper for fingerprints. There were none on it.

She was still puzzled as she laid the note down and began to change her clothes. As soon as she was dressed for the dig, Nancy went to the excavation and climbed down.

The busy workers looked up and said, "Hi!" Julie Anne asked if she had had any luck reaching Ned.

"Yes," Nancy replied. "I'll tell you about it later." She changed the subject and asked, "Which one of you left a note on the bureau?"

"Note?" Julie Anne repeated. "There wasn't any note when I was in the room."

Not only Nancy's roommates but all the other girls said they knew nothing about the message that had been left for Nancy.

"How about you boys?" Nancy called out.

They in turn denied having written it. Art asked, "What did it say?"

Nancy told him and the others. Theresa looked disturbed. "This is serious. I beg of you, if anyone here did it as a joke, please own up so none of us will be worried." The whole group reiterated that they knew nothing about the strange message.

"Oh, Nancy," Julie Anne burst out, "it must have been that awful man or some pal of his!"

Theresa Bancroft said she did not like the thought of anyone sneaking around the dig. "Whoever the person is, he's very brazen to come here in the daylight. I want all of you to be very careful."

Nancy's roommates were alarmed over the situation. They were sure she had not heard the last of her enemy.

Julie Anne, after thinking this over, said, "I don't believe what's in that note. If the person had really found the message and was on the track of a treasure, he wouldn't bother to tell you. I think he left the note to frighten you away. If you don't leave, he may harm you."

Nancy turned to Theresa. "There's good logic in what Julie Anne says. I think I should go to Cairo and stay there until my friends arrive. Did Art tell you they're coming?"

"He didn't say a word," Julie Anne replied.

Art lowered his eyes. Was it possible he did not like the idea? Quickly Nancy explained about the five friends who would join her on the river trip.

"That's fine," said Theresa. "And bring them back with you after the trip. We've plenty of room. As for your leaving here today, I insist that you stay until it's time to go meet your friends."

The archaeologist requested that everyone get back to work. Nancy picked up her shovel.

The boys had unearthed the fine skeleton of a man and carried it to the laboratory. Here they planned to wire it together so it could be hung up and exhibited. When the others finished work, they all trooped to the barn to see it.

The skeleton was suspended from a rod which the boys had put up. Theresa was very much pleased and said it was one of the finest specimens ever to be uncovered.

"Any museum would be delighted to have this," she remarked, "but I'm glad it will be on exhibit at Paulson University."

After dinner Nancy invited Julie Anne to go on the towboat trip.

"Oh how exciting!" she exclaimed. "Suppose I ask Theresa right away."

She hurried off. On the way to find the leader, Julie Anne met Art who was about to make the same request. Both promised Theresa they would work doubly hard as soon as they returned to the dig.

"All right, go ahead," Theresa said. "Neither of you has been in this area before and it will be a nice side trip for you."

As usual the evening was gay with singing and for the time being everyone forgot about Nancy's mysterious note. Finally all the boys went home except Bob Snell, who remained on guard.

The girls fell asleep quickly but at once Nancy began having worrisome dreams. She could see pirates attacking towboats and barges. She spotted sneaking figures in the moonlight, and finally when someone tried to grab Père François's treasure from her, she woke up.

"Oh!" she said softly. "What a nightmare!"

Everything around her was peaceful but Nancy could not get back to sleep. Finally she arose, pulled on slacks and a shirt and went outdoors. She did not see Bob Snell and wondered where he was. Restless, she walked past the dig site and around the house to the farmyard.

The night was dark, with few stars, but her eyes soon became accustomed to this. She could make out the shape of the old barn. Beyond it lay the wide empty field and the woods. Far in the distance a dog barked and another answered.

Nancy wondered where Bob was. Perhaps behind the barn-lab? She considered turning on her flashlight, but instinct told her not to.

"What's the matter with you?" she asked herself sternly. "You're actually nervous!"

The next moment she heard a low creaking noise. Someone was slowly opening the barn door! Instantly she knew it was not Bob. He would not be so cautious about it.

Before Nancy could investigate, a strange ghost-like shape appeared from the ramshackle building. Nancy's heart began to pound as she saw what it was. A skeleton was walking toward her!

Nancy blinked several times, then her good sense returned and she knew someone was carrying the skeleton in front of him.

He must be a thief! Walking on tiptoe but quickly, Nancy came up to the skeleton. Someone was indeed carrying it!

"Put that down!" she ordered, reaching out to grab the bony figure.

There was a startled grunt from behind the skeleton and the next moment a man thrust it at her, brushed past, and ran fast toward the road.

"Bob! Bob!" Nancy shouted, but got no reply.

She did not dare pursue the fugitive. It was too dangerous, and besides, she had retrieved the valuable fossil and must hold onto it.

"I'd better put this back in the lab."

As she was about to walk to the barn, two flashlights appeared from the farmhouse. Julie Anne was holding one, Theresa the other.

Seeing the skeleton, Julie Anne gave a loud squeal. Then, spotting Nancy, she exclaimed, "What on earth!"

Quickly Nancy explained and Theresa said, "I'm glad you didn't run after the man. Where's Bob?"

"I don't know," Nancy answered. "I called him but he didn't answer."

Julie Anne asked worriedly, "Do you think that thief might have knocked him out?"

"Oh, I hope not!" Theresa said. "We'll put the skeleton back in the lab and then hunt for Bob."

He was not in the big workroom nor anywhere else in the barn. The three searchers walked around the exterior of the farmhouse but did not find him.

"He may have become ill and gone to the boys' house," said Theresa. "We'd better go over and inquire."

She and Julie Anne hastened to their bedroom and slipped into some clothes. Then the three headed across the field to the boys' quarters.

Nancy knocked on the door and moments later Art answered, pulling on his robe. Seeing the girls, he was alarmed. "What's the matter?"

Nancy told him what had happened.

A skeleton was walking toward her!

"I'll check and see if Bob's here," said Art. In a few moments he came back to the door. "Not here," he reported grimly. "We'd better search."

"Yes," Theresa said anxiously. "He may have met with foul play."

In twenty minutes the field and woods were alive with flashlights as all the boys joined in the search for the missing youth.

At dawn they still had not found any sign of Bob. Everyone returned to the girls' farmhouse for a quick breakfast, then they started out on another search, this time by bright daylight.

Art wrinkled his brow. "It's odd. Bob would never go off without telling someone."

By this time all the searchers were sure that something had happened to him.

"He may have been attacked and carried off into the woods," Art suggested to Nancy and Julie Anne. "Let's look there."

The girls followed him onto an overgrown path among the trees. The three became silent as they looked intently for clues.

A few minutes later Art cried out, "Here's something!"

CHAPTER X

Disappearances

A torn piece of bright-patterned material had been stuck into the crotch of a tree near the path.

"This is from Bob's shirt, no doubt about it," Art told Nancy and Julie Anne.

Nancy examined the scrap and said she was sure it had not been snagged off, but deliberately torn and placed there by Bob.

"I believe he left it as a clue to where he was being taken—straight ahead."

Art went back to call the other searchers and soon the whole group was pounding down the trail. They could see various-sized footprints. Upon investigation, Nancy declared that besides Bob there had been two other men. The three had been together at first, then Bob had evidently dropped back, trying to escape. Unseen by them he had placed the cloth in the tree as a clue, in case he did not make it. His captors had run back and prodded him ahead.

"Poor Bob!" Julie Anne exclaimed. "He must have been overpowered."

"And probably gagged," Nancy added. "Otherwise he'd have yelled for help."

All agreed and hurried along the overgrown path. It was easy to follow the trail because grass had been trampled where no footprints were evident. Nancy and Art had outdistanced the others. As they turned a corner in the woods both of them could hear water running. In a few moments they came to a deep stream.

"Now what do we do?" Art asked.

Nancy gazed left and right. No footprints or trampled grass were visible. Had Bob been taken away in a boat?

Holding her hands binocular-fashion around her eyes, Nancy focused on the opposite bank and tried to detect possible footprints. She could see none.

"I'm afraid we're stopped for the time being," she said in disappointment. "Let's retrace our steps and keep looking for clues." They found nothing and in dismay returned to the dig.

"We must notify the State Police," Theresa remarked with mounting concern.

"I'll be glad to do it," Nancy spoke up. "That is, if Art will take me to town. And I want to phone home."

"I'll get the motorcycle."

He brought the vehicle to the front of the house and said to Nancy, "Hop aboard!"

As they neared Walmsley, Art said he thought they should call Bob's house before notifying the police.

"It's possible that he escaped from his captors and is home by now."

Nancy doubted this, but agreed it was a good thing to do. They went to the telephone booth they had used before and Art put in the call. Bob's father was shocked to hear the news. Not only had his son not come home, but he and Mrs. Snell had not heard from him since he had left for the dig site.

"This is alarming," Mr. Snell said to Art. "If I don't hear from Bob or the police soon, I'll notify the FBI. Bob may have been taken out of the state."

Art hung up. Then he dialed State Police Head-quarters and handed the phone to Nancy. She reported Bob's disappearance and the fact that the farmhouse near the dig had been visited more than once by an intruder or intruders. "The one last night tried to steal a skeleton," she said.

"We'll look into this whole matter at once," the officer promised. "Men will come to the dig. And if you get any more clues, be sure to let us know."

Nancy agreed to do this and said good-by. As

she paused before making her next call, Art asked, "Phoning your dad?"

Nancy shook her head. "I want to tell Ned about the arrangements for the towboat and barge trip."

Art walked off a little distance looking very glum. There was no doubt about it—he was jealous! Nancy hoped there would be no trouble between him and Ned.

It was fully a minute before she reached Ned. "Everything's set," she reported. "Julie Anne and Art and I will meet you tomorrow afternoon at the Delta Motel in Cairo. Toward suppertime we'll go aboard the towboat. It's called the *Sally O.*"

"Sounds great!" Ned replied. "I'll get in touch with the others right away. It sure will be good to see you again, Nancy. It's been a long time."

Nancy smiled. It had been only two weeks! But she was delighted that Ned felt this way and replied, "Yes, it has seemed like ages."

After she had finished talking to him, Nancy phoned her own home. Her father was not around, so she told Hannah Gruen the news, including the disappearance of Bob Snell.

"That's dreadful," the Drews' housekeeper said, then gave a great sigh. "Nancy, every place you go, it seems as if mysteries just pile up one after another."

"I guess you're right, Hannah dear," the young

detective replied. "All of us are terribly worried about Bob. We think he was kidnapped, but nobody can figure out why. There's been no ransom demand. His family hasn't a great deal of money, anyway, and certainly Bob doesn't."

"I'll be thinking good thoughts for him," Hannah said. "Let me know the minute he's found."

Hannah also reported that Mr. Drew had been away overnight and would not return until that evening.

Nancy said to give him her love, then went to join Art. Riding back to the dig, he seemed lost in thought. She wondered if he was worrying about Bob Snell or just being foolishly jealous of Ned.

"Would you mind stopping at Clem Rucker's farm?" she inquired. "I asked to have messages for me sent in care of him at the Walmsley post office. There might be one or two."

Art turned onto a side road and the couple bounced along until they reached the elderly farmer's house. He was just coming in from the fields.

"Howdy, folks," he greeted them. "Nancy, I went to the post office this mornin' and picked up a couple o' letters for you. Figgered to bring 'em over later. Wait a minute. I'll get 'em."

He disappeared inside the house but was back in a few seconds with Nancy's mail. She asked if he and Art would mind if she read them.

"No. Go ahead," Clem answered. "I reckon you're curious."

Nancy tore open one of the envelopes. The letter inside was from Roscoe Thompson, the helicopter pilot. He would come to the dig at eleven o'clock the next morning to pick up his three passengers. Nancy reported this to Art, who smiled feebly.

The other letter was from Mr. Drew. In it he told of a telephone conversation with his sister in New York. Aunt Eloise had given him some startling news.

The letter read:

"Boycey Osborne is very much concerned about one of his colleagues who was on the detective club trip. This man, A. C. E. Armstrong, left the group to go visit a brother in Rochester, New York. Now Boycey has learned that Armstrong never arrived there. No one has heard from him since he left his friends in Illinois. A search of hospitals has failed to reveal his whereabouts.

"Everyone is extremely worried that Armstrong met with foul play. If you come upon any clues, Nancy, get in touch with Boycey immediately."

Shocked, Nancy read the letter aloud. Art and Clem were disturbed by the news.

"Do you suppose," Art asked, "that he might have been kidnapped and there's some connection between his disappearance and that of Bob Snell?"

"But they didn't know each other," Nancy replied, "and they were on different projects."

Clem wanted to hear more regarding Bob Snell, so they told him the whole story. The farmer said he would certainly keep his eyes open for clues.

When Nancy and Art arrived at the farmhouse, the others were already eating lunch under the trees. The couple reported what they had learned. The girls were aghast at the story of the disappearance of A. C. E. Armstrong and a few of them hinted about going home before the situation became more dangerous.

"I can't say I blame you," Theresa replied. "But you couldn't go before tomorrow. I suggest that hereafter we have guards at both houses day and night."

"May I make a suggestion?" Nancy asked. "There must be some whistles in camp. Why don't we use them to alert one another at a moment's notice?"

"A very good idea," Theresa agreed.

Only two whistles were found. At supper these were given to the two boys who would act as guards that night. Les Blake was to stand watch at the girls' farmhouse.

"Don't hesitate to whistle if you see anything suspicious," Theresa told him as she and the girls went into the house at bedtime.

Nancy and Julie Anne packed their clothes in

preparation for the take-off the following morning. Finally they got to bed and all the lanterns and flashlights were extinguished.

Some time later Nancy was awakened by the shrill sounds of a whistle. For a moment she could not figure out why it was being blown, then suddenly she remembered. Les Blake was warning them of danger!

The other girls had also been awakened. With Nancy leading them, they hurried to the door, beaming flashlights.

CHAPTER XI

Problem in Jealousy

As the girls rushed from the farmhouse, a bright light was turned on them, almost blinding the group. They could hear running footsteps.

"What happened?" Julie Anne asked excitedly.

At that moment the glaring light was switched away from them and focused onto two fleeing figures. All the girls beamed their own flashlights and now could see Les who carried a powerful electric lantern. He made no attempt to dash after the men so Nancy hurried up to him.

"Let's catch them!" she suggested, and started to run.

Les held her back. "No, it's too dangerous. Those men were going to kidnap you!"

"What!" cried Julie Anne who had rushed to their side.

Les explained that he had seen two figures approaching the house and hidden himself behind a bush to watch them. They had paused near him to talk in whispers.

Les went on, "I heard one of them say, 'I've been casing the place. I know which is the Drew girl's bed. You wait here. I'll go in and put her in a deep sleep and carry her out.'

" 'Right,' the other man said. 'She's been interfering with our plans long enough.' Then the first man said, 'Okay, Kit.' "

Nancy and Julie Anne gasped. The other girls had crowded around and were exclaiming how dreadful it was.

"This place is really getting dangerous!" Claire Warwick said, eyeing Nancy scornfully.

Nancy had to agree and was sure now that she was the cause of it all. Perhaps she should not come back here after the towboat trip, but instead find some secret place to stay while she worked on the hollow oak mystery.

She asked Les to describe the men. The one who was called Kit fitted the description of the man who said his name was Tom Wilson. As before, he did not limp.

"But who was his companion?" Nancy wondered.

Les said he had decided at first to jump out at the men with his lantern and scare them away, but then realized he would be no match for them in a fight.

"I'm sorry we lost those would-be kidnappers," he remarked.

Nancy thanked him. Forcing a smile, she said to the others, "Tomorrow morning I'll be leaving and all your worries will be over."

"I'm glad to hear that," Claire Warwick said. "I mean no offense, Nancy, but after all you're not an archaeology student and your detective work here has—"

"That will be enough," Theresa spoke up sharply. "I suggest that all you girls go back to bed."

Claire looked angry and mumbled something about being treated like a child. But she followed the others into the house and went to her room.

Julie Anne put an arm around Nancy. "Don't let her worry you, dear. Nobody cares for Claire and I'm sure all the other girls like you. They'd be sorry to see you leave for good."

Nancy smiled in appreciation. She slept a few hours, then was up before the rising bell.

When the boys arrived from their house, they were astounded to learn of the attempted kidnapping. Art said, "I wonder if the same two men took Bob Snell away."

"If so, I'm pretty sure I know who one of them is," Nancy told him, and mentioned Kit Kadle, alias Tom Wilson. "It's a good thing we're going on the towboat trip for a few days. Maybe Kadle will think I've gone home and the group here won't be harassed by intruders."

Art made no comment. As he looked off into space, Nancy wondered, "Can he still be sulking about meeting Ned?" They walked into the farmhouse and joined the line for a cafeteria breakfast. Art ate quickly and went back to his dormitory to pack. The others did not see him until a quarter to eleven when he trudged up the path carrying a suitcase.

Nancy and Julie Anne were waiting for the helicopter to arrive. As the three looked up, they could see it coming. In a few minutes the whirlybird settled down onto the field near the farmhouse.

The trio hurried forward to greet Roscoe Thompson. Nancy introduced Julie Anne, then the three passengers climbed the ladder into the cockpit. The pilot asked how everything had been going and was told there had been trouble at the dig.

Nancy reported the disappearance of Bob Snell, suggesting that while Roscoe was flying around the area, he might keep his eyes open for anything suspicious.

"I'll do that. But why would anyone want to kidnap him?"

"Nobody knows," Art answered.

Nancy did not intend to mention her own danger, but Julie Anne blurted it out.

Roscoe's eyes opened wide. "This is pretty bad," he remarked. "You're lucky those two fellows didn't succeed."

"I agree," Nancy said. "I believe you know one of the men as Tom Wilson."

Roscoe looked surprised. "Is that so? But Wilson limps. How come you couldn't catch him?"

Art chuckled. "He had a limp until he was cornered and then he could run like a deer."

By this time the copter was coming in for a landing at a private field outside of Cairo. Roscoe borrowed a pilot friend's car and drove his three passengers to town. When he pulled up to the entrance of the Delta Motel, they said good-by and went inside.

Art and the girls checked their luggage, then had a light lunch. Nancy suggested that they take a taxi to the airfield and meet Ned and the others. During the ride Art did not say a word. When they reached the field he walked off by himself.

"What's eating him?" Julie Anne asked.

"Competition," Nancy replied. "Julie Anne, I think you'll have to cheer up poor Art."

The girl beamed. "Do you think I can do it? He's been tagging after you ever since you arrived."

"Of course you can," Nancy said. "Why don't you start in right now by walking over to him?"

Julie Anne liked this idea and set off at once. Nancy strolled up and down but kept an eye on the couple. Pretty soon she was delighted to see that Art was actually laughing. When the helicopter from St. Louis hove into sight he took Julie Anne's arm and brought her over to where Nancy was standing.

There was wild enthusiasm as Nancy greeted Bess and George and the boys. Julie Anne, meanwhile, had rushed up to her cousin Ned and hugged him. Then she introduced him to Art. The two shook hands and Ned was most cordial, but Art seemed aloof.

There was a lot of chatter on the way to the motel. The newcomers were shocked when they heard about the mysterious happenings at the dig, and the two disappearances plus the attempted kidnapping of Nancy.

Burt, blond and husky, said, "I wish I'd been here to capture those two guys."

Dave, a green-eyed rangy blond, added, "Pretty bold guys!"

Both Bess and George expressed their deep concern for Nancy.

"Maybe you're not safe anywhere around here," Bess added.

Nancy, happy at being reunited with her friends, laughed it off. "Kit Kadle would have to be the world's best swimmer to get out to the towboat. I understand swimming in the Ohio is dangerous because of step-offs and strong undercurrents."

Presently the group reached the motel and the new arrivals added their bags to the other luggage. Together the eight visitors strolled around the small town. Many of the houses were modest frame structures, but on a lovely tree-lined street they found several Victorian mansions.

One stately red-brick house was open for inspection and they took the tour. As they walked through the handsome high-ceilinged rooms, Bess kept her eye on Art. It had not taken her long to realize that the young man had become very fond of Nancy and resented Ned's being there. She was intrigued at the way he found excuses to speak to Nancy whenever Ned was not nearby.

At first Ned did not seem to notice this, but he soon realized the situation. From then on the two boys did not say a word to each other.

"Hm!" Bess thought. "Here's a problem in jealousy!"

She decided to do something about it. While they were admiring the silver tea service in the dining room, Bess said to Art, "Julie Anne is a great girl, don't you think?"

"Why—uh—yes," he answered.

Nancy overheard the remark and was fearful something unpleasant might happen to ruin the trip. Quickly she interrupted.

"Art likes everybody, so it's hard for him to be nicer to one person than another."

The young man paused a moment. "I guess that's right," he replied and walked off.

Nancy took Bess aside. "Please don't say any more. Apparently you've seen a little tension here. I'm hoping Art will pay more attention to Julie Anne, but I can't rush it."

Bess nodded. "I wouldn't want to start anything for the world."

Nancy and her friends had an early dinner at a small restaurant, then hailed a taxi. They picked up their luggage and the boys' sleeping bags, and rode to the riverfront. A tugboat took them out a short distance to a white towboat with red trim. How spick and span it looked!

A broad-shouldered man with a ruddy face met them on a narrow deck and helped the girls aboard. "Welcome to the *Sally O*," he said. "I'm Captain Boge."

Ned introduced the visitors, and the captain led them into a galley. A pretty, middle-aged woman in a pink housedress was taking a pan of hot rolls from a shiny oven.

"This is our cook Mattie," said the captain.

The woman chuckled. "I'm everything," she said. "Housemother and nurse, too. If you want anything let me know. And help yourselves to cake and fruit any time." She pointed to the food on the side counter.

"Oh, my diet!" moaned Bess.

The captain led his passengers to an upper

deck and showed them a deluxe double bedroom with its own adjoining lounge and bath.

"This is for the girls," he said. "You boys will use your sleeping bags on the afterdeck." He grinned. "If it rains you can duck into the engine room."

"This is great," said George. "I never knew towboats were so beautiful."

After freshening up and changing to pants suits, the girls joined the boys in the pilot house. Captain Boge was there. Before they could speak to him, the boat was suddenly shaken by a terrific jolt.

"Nothing to worry about," the captain assured them. "We're shaping up, that's all."

From the wide front window he pointed to a tugboat maneuvering the huge barges into position. Fascinated, the visitors watched the sure-footed crew roping them securely together.

"We call this wiring 'em up," said the captain. "It takes a long time because we have to be sure they all fit together and will ride without bucking."

At twilight the job was finished. The towboat started slowly upstream, pushing fifteen barges ahead of it, three abreast. Some were empty, others filled with grain and coal.

Looking behind, the boys noted where the blue-gray water of the Ohio met the muddy Mississippi. "That's quite a sight," Dave remarked.

Ahead were low tree-lined banks. Soon these vanished into darkness.

Here and there the young people saw the lights of small towns or a brilliantly lighted cement plant on the shore. Now and then the red and green lights of another boat approached and the captain blew a deafening blast on his horn. At midnight the weary passengers went to bed.

Around noon the next day Captain Boge said they were near Cave in Rock. He pointed out a quarry on the Illinois shore. "I'm leaving my bow barges off there, and taking on two others, so I'll be tied up a couple of hours. If you want to visit the cave, go out to that first barge and jump off when it's against the dock." He gave them directions to the rocky cavern.

The visitors followed his advice and walked along the edge from one barge to another until they came to the end. When this barge was maneuvered into place, the passengers jumped off and started for Cave in Rock. They walked along the tree-lined bank. When it became rocky they climbed upward and soon emerged from the woods a few yards from the mammoth cave.

Nancy suddenly put up her hand for everyone to halt. "Listen!" she said. "I think I hear a cry for help."

CHAPTER XII

Rewarding Search

As the eight friends stood listening, the cry was repeated.

"That sounds as if it came from up there somewhere," said Nancy. She pointed to the top of the bluff above the cave.

The group hurried up a series of stone steps at one side of the huge opening to the cliff top. Nobody was around.

The searchers fanned out and looked in the surrounding woods but found no one, and finally met again at the foot of the steps.

"Somebody else may have discovered the person who needed help," Nancy suggested.

Ned looked at her searchingly. "Do you suppose the cry was made to get us up to the bluff and keep us away from Cave in Rock until someone who didn't want to be seen got out of there?"

Nancy agreed that this was possible. "But how could anyone know we were coming?" she asked.

Just then they saw a boy of fourteen racing across the top of the cliff and yelling. Apparently he was shouting to a friend.

"There's the answer," Nancy commented, then added, "Let's have a look at the cave now."

Following her and Ned, they all climbed up to the wide clearing in front of the huge cave mouth.

"I can see why this was a great place for pirates," Dave declared. "It's halfway between the bluff top and the river. With a lookout up on the cliff nobody could take them by surprise."

When the young people entered the shadowy cavern, their voices resounded strangely. They walked up the gradually sloping floor toward the rear.

"I've read about this place," said Julie Anne. "Prehistoric Indians used it, too. And in 1831 the cave was the hideout for a gang of counterfeiters."

Bess shivered. "And now maybe Nancy's enemies are staying in it."

"They couldn't have been here long," Ned remarked. "After all, this is a public park and people come and go."

"We seem to be the only ones around here right now," said George.

"Let's look for the treasure," Nancy urged, "and keep our eyes open for any clues to Kit

Kadle, or anything pertaining to the hollow oak."

Nancy and Ned took out flashlights and the intensive hunt began. There was no hidden treasure in sight.

"I've a hunch we're wasting our time following up the legend Lightfoot told me," Nancy said. "Maybe river pirates did rob Père François, but it seems unlikely any would have been around here in his day. I recall now that the only travelers were the Indians and a few explorers and trappers."

Ned agreed. "It was more than a hundred years later that lots of pioneers headed westward. Many floated down the Ohio on flatboats with all their possessions. That was when piracy flourished."

"Lightfoot," Nancy remarked, "probably confused Père François's story with some other legend."

Nevertheless she beamed her light over the walls once more. Seconds later she caught sight of something just out of reach. It was a piece of paper sticking out slightly from a crevice between rocks. She called to six-foot Ned to pull it out.

"But be careful," she said. "It looks fragile."

Ned reached up and little by little he pried out a folded sheet of paper, which he handed to Nancy.

"This sure is dirty and ready to fall apart," he said.

It was evident the paper had been subjected to

dampness and dirt and there were holes in it here and there. Nancy unfolded it gingerly and played her flashlight on the faint writing. The smudgy message was hard to read and part was missing, but the young detective's heart leaped excitedly when she saw the signature.

"It says A. C. E.!" she exclaimed. "I'm sure this was written by A. C. E. Armstrong, Boycey Osborne's friend."

Ned asked, "What does the note say?"

Nancy read it aloud:

> " 'Prisoner of Kit Ka
> Tak   me to cell
> in El   town.' "

By this time all the others in the cave had gathered around Nancy and asked if she could decipher the meaning. She studied the paper a few moments, then replied, "I believe the whole message is:

> " 'Prisoner of Kit Kadle.
> Taking me to cellar
> in Elizabethtown.' "

"You're a wonder!" Art exclaimed and immediately came close to Nancy.

She smiled but made no comment. Instead she said enthusiastically, "Now I have a real clue for Boycey!"

The whole group went outside and sat down to discuss the message.

Julie Anne asked, "How are we going to get to Elizabethtown?"

"Our towboat passed that town about seven miles back," Ned spoke up. "We'll probably have to leave the *Sally O*."

"We'd better hustle to the boat or it will leave us!" Burt remarked.

"Oh, I'm sure Captain Boge wouldn't abandon us," said Bess.

"That's true," Nancy agreed, "but it's not fair to keep him waiting."

She tucked the precious note into a pocket and hurried with her friends to the quarry dock. As soon as Nancy was on board, she and Ned reported their discovery to Captain Boge.

"We should go to Elizabethtown, so I'm afraid we must end our trip now," she said.

"That won't be necessary," the captain replied with a wry smile. "We've developed engine trouble and are going to be here quite a while, I'm afraid. You can have the rest of the afternoon for your search, but be back by six o'clock. I'm hoping to be able to take off then."

"How'll we get to Elizabethtown?" Ned asked.

"Maybe somebody from the quarry will be driving there," he said. "I'll see."

Stepping out of the pilot house onto the landing of an iron stairway, the captain called down to a man on the dock. After a short conversation Boge came back inside.

"All set," he said. "You can go in with that fellow in about ten minutes if you don't mind riding in a pickup truck."

"That's okay with us," said Nancy. "Is there anything we can do for you while we're there?"

"You could pick up several chocolate bars at the general store," the captain said. "The crew likes them."

Nancy and Ned hurried off to tell their friends about the trip. Quarter of an hour later the young people were seated in the back of a green pickup truck bouncing along a narrow road toward Elizabethtown. When they reached the main street of the small town, the driver let them out.

"Where is the police station?" Nancy asked.

The man chuckled. "We don't need one. There's only one policeman—he's the marshal. But he's away on vacation. Go up this side street," he said, pointing to a tree-shaded lane, "to the third house. That's where Ben Wooster lives. He's the marshal's deputy right now." The young people thanked the driver and he went off.

It was agreed that Nancy and Ned would talk to the deputy while the others did the shopping and went sightseeing around the tiny town. A short distance away they could see a small, attractive park overlooking the river front.

"We'll meet there at five o'clock," Ned told them.

He and Nancy hurried off to the deputy's house.

A thin, red-haired young man was seated on the porch steps eating an apple.

"Are you Deputy Wooster?" Nancy asked.

"I am," he said solemnly. "What's the trouble?" He pointed to the steps. "Take a seat."

The couple did, and after introducing themselves, quickly explained about the kidnapped detective. Nancy showed Mr. Wooster the note she had found in the cave.

"Well, now, the marshal told me about this Kit Kadle and the two fellows he probably kidnapped," said the officer, "but this is the first lead we've had to them. Trouble is," he added thoughtfully, "this is a mighty small town—only five hundred folks or so and I know just about all o' them. I can't think o' anybody who would have a man hidden in his cellar or anywhere else, for that matter."

"Is there an empty house around?" Nancy asked.

The young man raised his sparse eyebrows. "Now there you may have a squirrel in the tree, young lady. The old Hatchett house has been empty for almost five years."

"'Tain't empty now," said a raspy voice.

Nancy turned to see a skinny blond youth in dungarees coming up the walk.

"This is my cousin Jimmy," said the deputy. "He lives next door and he don't miss much."

"I think somebody's livin' in the Hatchett

place," the newcomer went on, "Hank and me were out that way in our car a couple o' nights ago and saw lights in the house and a car in the driveway."

Deputy Wooster stood up. "I'd better look into this," he said firmly. He reached into a trouser pocket, took out a badge, and pinned it to his blue shirt.

"Is there trouble?" Jimmy asked, his blue eyes sparkling. "Can I go with you, Ben?"

"Okay," said the deputy. "I guess we could use an extra man. But it might be dangerous. You do only what I tell you." He turned to Nancy and Ned. "Did you folks have lunch?"

"A little," Nancy replied.

"Jimmy," said the deputy, "go in the kitchen and fetch some apples and that bag o' doughnuts on the table. I'll start the car."

A few minutes later Nancy and Ned were riding in the back seat of the police car. The deputy drove down a dirt road outside of town. Jimmy shared the apples and doughnuts with them as they told him about the note. After several turns, Wooster headed along a rutted lane and pulled off into a small clearing.

"We'll walk from here," he said quietly.

Single file, the four made their way up the road, keeping inside the tree line. At the edge of a driveway they stopped.

"Wow!" Ned exclaimed. "What a wreck!"

Before them was a large gray frame house with broken shutters and a tumble-down porch.

"No car in the driveway now," Nancy noted. "I can't believe anyone is living in this place."

The four circled the old dwelling but saw no signs of life. Then they walked carefully onto the sagging porch. The front door was standing ajar. Quietly they entered.

"Let's try the cellar," Nancy urged. She took out her flashlight and the deputy turned on his.

"It's that door at the end of the hall," whispered Jimmy. "I explored this place a couple o' years ago."

As noiselessly as possible they went down the dark stairway. Except for a huge furnace and some odds and ends of junk the cellar was empty.

"Where were the lights you saw?" Nancy asked Jimmy.

"Upstairs."

Carefully the group searched the first floor, then climbed to the second. While Wooster and his cousin were examining the bedrooms, Nancy and Ned spotted a door which they suspected might lead to a third-floor attic. Ned opened it and the two listened. There was a stairway indeed but everything above was dark.

Nancy and Ned started up the steps. Suddenly they stopped. From somewhere ahead of them came the sound of heavy breathing.

CHAPTER XIII

Alarming Moments

"Somebody's up there!" Nancy whispered to Ned.

The two hurried up the stairway and Nancy beamed her flashlight over the dark attic.

A man was lying on the floor, bound and gagged!

The couple rushed over to the prisoner and released him. He smiled weakly and whispered, "Thank you. How did you know I was here?"

Without replying to his question, Nancy asked, "Are you A. C. E. Armstrong?"

"Yes."

At that moment Ben Wooster and Jimmy hurried into the attic. They stared in disbelief.

"You found him!" exclaimed the deputy. "Are you all right, mister?"

"I think so," Armstrong said hoarsely.

The deputy shook his head. "It's amazin'. I'll drive you to a doctor in town right away. He can look you over and send you to a hospital if need be. Take it easy. Jimmy, get the car."

While the youth was gone, Nancy asked A.C.E. about his abduction, adding that she had received the news of his disappearance from her aunt. "Your detective friends will be relieved to learn you've been found."

"I was waylaid in my car," he began, "by Kit Kadle and another man soon after I left the hollow oak area. They were armed and said if I didn't tell them where the tree was with the message in it, they would kill me.

"Of course I couldn't tell them because I didn't know myself. Kadle had assumed that since the other members of the detective club had left for New York, they had solved the mystery and knew where the treasure was, but hadn't had time to dig it up."

"You're sure there is a treasure?" Ned questioned Armstrong. "And that it's buried?"

"No, I'm not sure. Kadle assumed that the message would tell where a treasure was buried. They took me in my car to a shack in a woods, then to the cave and finally here."

Nancy told him about finding the note in the cave. "Why did the men take you there?"

"They had to meet another man, and I guess they were afraid to leave me alone. We arrived late in the afternoon and hid until after the park grounds closed. The third man must have done the same. When it was dark they met at the cave. I didn't get a good look at him nor hear his name. While the three were talking together I managed to write that note and stick it in the crack."

The deputy spoke up. "How long is it since you've seen Kadle and his pals?"

A.C.E. told them one or another of the men came to feed him three times a week. "Someone's due today so maybe you can catch him."

"I'll radio the State Police," Wooster said.

Ned asked A.C.E. if he knew Kadle was bothering the people at the dig, especially Nancy, and that he had planned to kidnap her.

"Yes, I was aware of all that," he replied. "I felt so helpless here when all I wanted to do was escape and expose Kadle."

"Did you know," Nancy queried, "that one of the boys at the dig disappeared and we suspect he too was kidnapped by Kadle and another man?"

A.C.E. said he had not heard the men say anything about this. "Ordinarily they talked freely in front of me and I have a feeling that sooner or later they were going to kill me so I couldn't expose them."

As Armstrong stopped speaking, Jimmy came pounding up the attic stairs. He, Ned, and the deputy helped the weakened man down to the car. On the way to town he expressed his thanks to Nancy and Ned for rescuing him.

"We're glad you're safe," said Nancy. She promised to call her Aunt Eloise, who would pass the news on to his family and friends.

After A.C.E. had been taken to the doctor, Nancy hurried off to make her call to New York. Miss Drew was thrilled to hear what had happened. Then Nancy met Ned, Ben Wooster, and Jimmy outside the physician's office.

"Mr. Armstrong will be okay," the deputy reported. "He'll rest here a couple o' days, then fly home. I've reported his car stolen. You young people did a great job today. Can I give you a lift somewhere?"

Nancy glanced at her watch. "It's nearly six o'clock," she said. "We have to get back to the towboat. But there are eight of us. We can't all fit in your car, I'm afraid."

"We'll take two cars," Jimmy offered eagerly. "I'll get mine!" He raced away.

Ned hurried to the waterfront park to round up the rest of their group. Nancy and Ned explained what had happened, then the group set off for the quarry dock.

When they reached the towboat, Nancy and her friends thanked Wooster and Jimmy and hurried on board.

"Just in time!" called Captain Boge from the pilot house. "The engine's fixed and we're ready to go!" The boat got under way.

After freshening up, the young people hurried to the dining area adjoining the galley. The table was set with a red-checked cloth and loaded with delicious-looking food.

"Oh!" gasped Bess. "It's like a beautiful dream! I had such a skimpy sandwich for lunch!"

The captain appeared and seated himself. Immediately the others did too. While the steaming bowls and platters were being passed around the table, Nancy and Ned told Captain Boge about finding the kidnapped man.

The captain was impressed. "So I have real detectives on board," he said. "That calls for extra big helpings of strawberry shortcake."

When Mattie brought in the heaping desserts, everyone praised her excellent cooking.

"I really can't eat another bite," said Bess, starting on the whipped cream.

They had just finished the dessert when there was a loud crash of glass and a log whizzed through a window, sailed over their heads, and landed against the far wall.

"Oh!" screamed Bess and everyone ducked.

The diners sat frozen to their chairs, and Mattie came to the door, pale and speechless.

Dave exclaimed, "What a narrow escape!"

Everywhere lay broken glass, some of which had showered those at the table. Burt had a small cut on one hand, but otherwise there were no injuries.

"We're lucky to be alive," George murmured.

When the shock of the incident passed, everyone jumped up and carefully shook off the glass.

The log sailed over their heads

Captain Boge said he was sorry about the accident, but glad his passengers were all right.

"Sometimes," he explained, "a floating log gets caught beneath a barge and is carried along underwater. When it breaks loose, the log is propelled upward with great force. It sometimes angles for the boat and crashes onto the deck."

George said grimly, "There was great force all right. If that had hit—"

Dave finished her remark. "— Lil ole me, Emerson would have lost a great football player. And it certainly couldn't afford that."

His facetiousness made everyone relax. The boys offered to put new glass in the window, while the girls sorted out the debris from the dishes and table linen. A deck hand would clean the floor, the captain told them.

When the work was finished, the young people gathered on deck and talked over the day's adventures. Nancy said that now she knew Kadle had not found the message in the hollow oak, she wanted to get back and pursue her search.

"I'm all for that," Art spoke up.

So much had been going on that the subject of jealousy between him and Ned had been forgotten. Nancy was happy over this and hoped the good relationship would last.

She approached Captain Boge and asked when they would get back to Cairo. He looked at her understandingly.

"I know you want to return to the dig soon but you'll have to be patient. During the night I'll be dropping off these barges at various stops. In the morning I'll pick up some at Uniontown, Kentucky, and start downstream. We'll be back in Cairo late the following day."

He smiled. "Then I'll go on down the Mississippi to New Orleans where I came from and you'll go back to your mystery."

During the evening the young people sat around the pilot house eating snacks and listening to Captain Boge.

"Lots of places on the Ohio have odd names," he said. "Like Dead Man's Island or Tobacco Patch Light or Lovers' Leap Light."

"That last one is romantic," said Bess, who was finishing her second apple.

Next morning the travelers gathered in the pilot house after breakfast to watch the new barges being put into place.

The captain pointed to a big one loaded with coal. "It's the last," he said. "When that jumbo is in place we'll be on our way."

"I'd love to get closer and watch," George said.

"Let's all go," Burt urged.

"Okay," said the captain. "But be careful."

With George in the lead, the young people hurried down the iron steps, across the deck and stepped out onto the middle barge. They walked quickly along from one to the other until they came to the front. A tugboat was maneuvering the loaded jumbo toward a bow barge. Several men stood at the end of it ready to rope the oncoming one into place.

George was already at the brink, leaning forward so as not to miss any of the procedure. At that moment they all felt a great jolt. George lost her balance and went down between the barge on which they had gathered and the oncoming one!

Julie Anne screamed. "Oh, George will be crushed!"

CHAPTER XIV

Bess's Scheme

NED had noticed a long boat hook lying on the deck. He picked it up quickly and with Dave's help held the two barges apart. It was hard work and they strained every muscle. Meanwhile the shouts of the boatmen had alerted the tug operator to cut his motor. The others looked around anxiously for George.

"There she is!" Nancy exclaimed in relief as her friend surfaced some distance away. George had swum underwater to safety.

"She's coming this way!" Bess cried.

The young people rushed to the side of the barge. George was an excellent swimmer and managed to get back despite a strong current. Luckily the barge was heavily loaded and rode low in the water. The boys reached down and hauled her aboard. George's clothes were dripping and her hair was as flat and shiny as a sleek cat's.

The girl grimaced. "Wasn't that stupid of me?"

The others made no comment, but Bess exclaimed, "Thank goodness you're all right!"

"Yes," added Burt. "You had a narrow squeak."

The men on the two barges involved set up a cheer upon seeing that George was safe. One of them called, "You're some swimmer, young lady!"

George held up her two hands in a thank-you gesture. Accompanied by Bess, Nancy and Julie Anne, she went to her cabin for dry clothes.

The boys stayed to see the rest of the operation. Soon the two barges were lashed together. The journey back to Cairo began.

About noontime they entered a lock beside the Kentucky shore. Intrigued, the young people stood at the rail watching the towboat slowly and skillfully push the triple line of barges between the concrete walls.

"The captain has to be good," said Ned. "He doesn't have much clearance on either side."

"That's for sure," said a man, standing on the wall. He wore a yellow hardhat.

"You're an Army Engineer, aren't you?" Art asked him. "I know your Corps is in charge of dams and locks."

"That's right," the man replied.

As they all chatted with the engineer, the *Sally*

O and her tow slowly sank lower between the walls.

Finally, far ahead, the great gates swung open and the *Sally O* rode out into the river. As the towboat passed through the opening, several other engineers waved from the lock wall.

Immediately afterward Nancy sought out Captain Boge. She asked if he could radio the Illinois State Police to find out if they had any word on Bob Snell or if Kadle or any of his gang had been caught at the old house.

"I guess we'd all like to know," Boge said.

He turned to his radio and made the call. To Nancy's disappointment, she heard the answering officer give negative replies to both queries.

Nancy went back to the deck and relayed the depressing news to the others. "Hypers!" George exclaimed. "Where *is* Bob Snell?"

A few minutes later luncheon was served. There had been no regular seating arrangements. The young people had moved around freely but Bess had noticed that whenever possible Art had placed himself next to Nancy. Later she mentioned this to Nancy, who laughed it off.

"Don't laugh," Bess said. "It's serious. I was hoping Art was going to stick close to Julie Anne but that didn't last long. I'm going to do something about this!"

Nancy begged her not to. Bess said no more,

but Nancy noticed that all afternoon she made a point of searching out Art and talking with him.

"Dave isn't going to like this one bit," Nancy thought. "Oh dear! Why can't things run along smoothly?"

Ned and Art stayed far apart. Nancy kept moving around to talk to everyone but little by little a strained air came over the whole group.

Apparently Captain Boge noticed this. At suppertime he said, "I want an honest answer to a question. Have you young folks been bored with this trip?"

"Oh no!" Nancy replied. "It's been full of excitement. How could we possibly be bored?"

The captain looked down at the table pensively. "You have all become so quiet I thought maybe something was wrong."

They all assured him he had nothing to worry about. The trip had been perfect. Apparently the captain decided to change the subject.

"Did you know a ghost can sometimes be seen at night walking on this river?"

George looked at him skeptically. "You're spoofing."

"You can decide for yourself," he said.

He told them that many years ago a young man and his sweetheart were coming down the river in a small sailboat. In a sudden freak wind the mainsail shifted so quickly it knocked the girl overboard.

"According to the story, she was never seen alive again, but her spirit appears on the water, hoping her lover will come back to her. If you watch the Illinois shore real closely, you might see her ghost tonight. Lots of folks say they have. I've never seen her, but tonight might be just the right time."

The young people did not believe a word of the legend, but they trooped to the deck in a more lighthearted mood than they had been in before. Nancy, Bess, and Captain Boge were pleased.

The whole group stayed up until midnight watching for the apparition, but did not see it. The next morning, however, Julie Anne declared she had been the girl ghost in her dreams.

"The young man in the boat who came to get me—was Art!" Everyone laughed and the other girls wondered if there were a double meaning in Julie Anne's remark.

The young people spent another pleasant day on the boat. At nightfall they saw the familiar shoreline of Cairo ahead.

They had already packed their bags and began saying good-by to the captain and crew. As the tugboat drew alongside to take them off the *Sally O,* the men gathered to wave.

Nancy lingered a moment to speak privately to Captain Boge. "Please don't worry about us. We honestly had a marvelous time and I assure you we're all good friends." The captain squeezed her hand understandingly and wished her well.

As soon as they reached the dock, Nancy asked Ned if he would mind telephoning Roscoe Thompson, the helicopter pilot. "Ask him to meet us at Cairo. We can taxi to the airfield."

The others waited for him. He rejoined them, smiling. "Roscoe will be there."

By the time the group reached the field, he was waiting for them. Nancy introduced him to Bess, George, Ned, Burt, and Dave.

"It'll be a tight squeeze," he said, "but we'll manage. It's not a long ride to the dig."

Before leaving, Nancy telephoned the State Police and learned there was no news of Bob Snell, and Kadle and his pals were still at large.

"I suppose they'll come to the dig," she thought. "We must keep our eyes open."

When the helicopter was airborne, Nancy asked Roscoe if he had done any searching from the air for Bob Snell.

"Yes, but I didn't spot anything suspicious. I sure hope somebody finds him soon."

As the helicopter set down, all the diggers heard it and ran out to greet Nancy and her friends. During the introductions and chatter that followed, Roscoe took off. Nancy immediately mentioned Bob Snell.

"His father came out here the day you left to meet your friends," Theresa said. "Mr. Snell is staying in Cairo and making his own investigation."

The newcomers were besieged with questions about the towboat trip and the treasure hunt.

Julie Anne and Art joined in giving answers. Everyone was glad to hear A.C.E. Armstrong had been rescued and thought it was clever of Nancy to have tracked him down.

"He was able to clear up a good bit of the mystery," she said. "We can start all over again looking for the message in the hollow oak."

The group went to the girls' farmhouse to hear the whole story over an evening snack. Afterward, Nancy saw Bess and Theresa walking up and down in front of the house together. The girl was talking animatedly and the director was nodding and smiling. Nancy wondered what the conversation was about, but Bess offered no explanation and Nancy did not prod her.

When it was time for the boys to leave, Nancy noticed that Art did not invite her friends to go with him. He stalked ahead alone. Todd took charge of them and they disappeared along the path leading to the boys' dormitory.

There were two extra beds in one of the girls' rooms. Bess and George were assigned to them.

Early the next morning when the boys arrived Art was on his motorcycle. Nancy explained to Theresa that she had asked him to go over to Clem Rucker's home and see if he would rent his farm truck to her. She planned on Ned's driving it in her search for the special oak tree.

Art roared off. He was back in a little while with the truck, the motorcycle lying in the rear. Sweet-smelling hay covered the board floor and Nancy was glad to see this, but knew it would hardly cushion the ride. It was not going to be a comfortable one.

It was a beautiful day and the whole group had breakfast outdoors. While they were eating, Nancy saw Theresa approach Julie Anne and speak to her quietly. The young detective noticed a look of disappointment cross Julie Anne's face.

Next the director walked over to Art and began to talk. He scowled but seemed to agree with Theresa. A few minutes later he came up to Nancy and said, "Sorry, but Theresa won't excuse me today. I have to dig."

Presently Julie Anne told Nancy their leader had made the same request of her. Nancy wondered if Bess had had a hand in this or whether Theresa had decided her students had had enough time off.

"I'll bet Bess is playing Cupid again," Nancy thought.

All her friends from home were intrigued by the excavation and went to watch the diggers at work. Julie Anne waved to them from below.

"Show us how you do it," Ned called to her.

She showed him, then suddenly said, "I've found part of a painted skull."

It was a slightly curved piece of reddish bone about two inches long.

"This is a good find," said Theresa. "It still bears traces of the red clay with which the Hopewell Indians painted the skulls of their dead."

"It could just as easily be an Algonquin skull," Claire said authoritatively. "I've heard they had some strange customs. Sometimes they mixed their bones into the burials of earlier people."

Theresa looked at the girl sharply. "That story is absolutely untrue. Where did you hear it?"

Cornered, Claire admitted that she had forgotten. "Then," said Theresa, "you should know better than to repeat such a story!"

Claire turned on her heel and walked away. Julie Anne winked at Nancy as if to say, "Little Miss Know-It-All didn't get away with it this time!"

Nancy told Theresa she and her group should leave at once to start their hunt. A box was quickly packed with sandwiches, fruit, cake, and bottles of soda. The three couples rode off in the open-back truck, with Ned at the wheel and Nancy beside him. She pointed out the direction, retracing the route Clem had taken.

Suddenly the sky grew dark. Large drops splashed against the windshield. There were cries from the riders in the back. A downpour followed and the narrow lane turned to slippery mud.

Nancy looked around frantically for shelter. Below, at the foot of a steep bluff, she spotted a tumble-down red frame building.

"There's an old railroad station!" she exclaimed. "We can go in there!"

Just then Ned swerved to avoid a boulder in the road. The heavy truck skidded out of control and slid down the muddy embankment straight for the old depot! There were screams from the rear.

"Hang on!" Ned yelled.

Crash!

The truck came to a halt with the cab inside the station. Plaster and boards rained down on it. The riders in the back scrambled out and hurried to the front.

"Nancy, Ned! Are you hurt?" George cried. Bess was white-faced with fright.

"We're all right, I guess," Nancy said shakily as she and Ned got out of the cab.

Ned gave a wry grin. "I don't think we did this old depot any good."

"It was a wreck to start with," said Burt.

The boys looked over the truck and found it undamaged. Meanwhile, Nancy searched the abandoned station on a hunch Bob Snell might be imprisoned there. She found only a broken cabinet in the ticket agent's office and a 1929 train schedule.

"It has stopped raining," said Bess.

"Then let's go!" Burt urged.

The girls found clean rags under the truck seat and wiped off the wet hay in the back. Then they all climbed in and Ned backed out of the broken wall. He drove along the grass-covered railroad tracks until he came to a gravel road leading back to the bluff.

Before long, Nancy recognized where they were. Straight ahead was the first hollow oak with the lead plate on it containing the name Père François, and the date, followed by an arrow. It was noon by the time they reached the area where the second tree was located. But it was on the other side of a deep creek.

"I guess we came out of our way," Nancy remarked.

"I'm starved!" said Bess. "Let's sit down here by this nice shady stream and have our lunch."

"Sounds good to me," Dave spoke up.

The three couples climbed out of the old truck and walked toward the water to wash their hands. Burt was the first to finish. As he turned back toward the truck he saw two little boys peering into the cab. Thinking they might know the best spot to drive across the stream, he hurried toward them. Instead of waiting for Burt, the two ran away as fast as they could.

"I guess they're shy of strangers," he thought with a smile, and waited for the others to join him.

Nancy, first to get there, reached into the cab for the box of food. The string which had been tied around it was gone. Quickly she took off the lid and looked inside.

"Oh no! It can't be!" she exclaimed.

CHAPTER XV

Strange Row of Stones

'At Nancy's outcry Bess looked into the box. She gave a little shriek. "What! No food?"

"Those little boys I saw running away," Burt remarked, "must have taken everything." He dashed off in the direction the children had taken.

Ned and Dave followed, while Bess sat down on the ground, disconsolate.

"Oh, don't be silly!" George chided her cousin. "It wouldn't hurt you to go without a meal."

"You're a good one to talk," Bess replied. "You eat all you want and stay slim. I can't help it if I get hungry."

It seemed like a long time before the boys returned. Ned was holding a package of sandwiches which the little boys had dropped. Burt and Dave had their hands filled with luscious raspberries. Streamers of watercress were trailing from their pockets.

"I see you retrieved some of our lunch," said Bess. "Did you catch those little monkeys?"

"No. They had too much of a head start, but if we ration this food, we won't starve."

Dave grinned. "I feel as if I'm on Operation Survival."

While they were eating, Nancy and her friends discussed how they were going to get across the water. They did not want to risk being trapped in midstream if the truck stalled.

"Let's follow the water upstream," Ned suggested. "We may come to a shallow place. We could cross there and then drive back to follow the direction of the arrow."

They started off but found the going a bit difficult. What had been a wagon road was now overgrown with grass and bushes. The truck was sturdy, however, and finally they came to a shallow part of the stream.

Nancy laughed. "I wonder if Clem knew about this road, but was in too much of a hurry to take this longer way."

She described the spill which she, Julie Anne, and Clem had taken when the farmer's old car had tipped over in the water.

When they reached the second hollow oak with the plate, Ned looked skeptically at the terrain due south. "We'd better not try taking this truck through those woods. I'm sure there's not enough space between the trees."

The whole group climbed out and waited for Nancy to lead the way. Everyone kept looking for hollow oaks, but found none. Finally they climbed to the top of a wooded ridge.

"Isn't that an old oak tree ahead of us?" George asked.

"It looks like one," Nancy replied. The six searchers hurried forward.

As they neared the tree, Ned remarked, "Somebody has mutilated this."

"But why?" Burt queried. "There's no lead plate on it and the tree looks pretty sturdy to me, not like one with a hollow center."

There was no doubt but that someone with a hatchet had hacked at the oak over and over again to get to the middle of it.

"The man who did this," said Burt, "must have thought it was the prize one."

"What a shame to damage it!" Bess said. "This was a gorgeous tree. Nancy, do you think the person who hacked the trunk has anything to do with the mystery?"

The young detective shrugged. "I'm not sure. He could have."

George spoke up. "If it was Kadle or his buddies they're probably getting so desperate to find the treasure that they'll hack any big oak."

Nancy wondered if the State Police had picked up Kadle or had any leads on him. She decided that before they returned to the dig she would go to Walmsley and find out whether there were any new developments.

The group trudged on down the side of the hill. According to the sun they were still going due south. Ahead was open farmland with a stretch of woods beyond. As they stumbled along over the uneven ground, Bess suddenly gave a cry and went down in a heap.

"Oh!" she exclaimed.

"What happened?" Dave asked, running to help her up.

"I stepped on a stone that moved," she said. "For a few seconds I thought I'd sprained my ankle, but it's okay." She stood up.

The others had come to see what had happened. Nancy, relieved to know her friend was all right, glanced down at the stone which had rocked under Bess's foot. Noting the odd shape, she picked it up and brushed off the dirt.

"It's a spearhead!" she exclaimed.

The others gathered closer to examine it.

"That looks like an old Indian relic," Dave remarked.

"I wonder," Nancy thought, "if someone put this on the ground to indicate a direction."

She decided it would be pure coincidence for the discovery to be associated with her mystery. But Nancy's detective instincts led her to hunt for more spearheads. A little farther on were a row of them. She pointed out her find to the others.

"They certainly mean something," Ned remarked. "And they all lead the same way."

"But," Burt objected," they couldn't possibly be directions to the hollow oak with the message in it. I think someone has put them here fairly recently."

"Why do you say that?" Bess asked.

"Because they're in such a neat line. If they'd been here for any length of time they'd have been disturbed by animals or people. Some would be missing, probably, or kicked out of order."

Nancy nodded. "Yes, I think so too."

All the young people wondered where the weaponheads had come from and who had placed them here. Suddenly into Nancy's mind sprang an image of Bob Snell. Could he possibly have done this, hoping that someone would find them and go the way they pointed? She was skeptical of this, however, telling herself Bob's abductors surely would not have given him time to place them.

She and her friends followed the spearheads for a few minutes. There were no clues to the missing student's whereabouts, nor to a hollow oak.

Nancy noticed that Bess was limping a bit and said they should go back. On the way she picked up three of the spearheads, while asking Bess, "Can you walk as far as the truck?"

"Oh yes," Bess replied. "But I'll be glad to get on level ground again!"

The boys helped her hop on the good foot and finally they all reached the truck. Nancy said she wanted to stop in Walmsley and telephone the State Police. She was not sure of the right direction, but she made a good guess and after a while they rode into town.

She called the police and told them about the spearheads. They were interested in her story and said they too would search the area.

"Incidentally nobody has come to that house where you found Mr. Armstrong. We think Kadle abandoned him or one of the gang was watching the place from the woods when Mr. Armstrong was taken away. If so, those kidnappers will not show up again in Elizabethtown."

"Maybe you'll have better news the next time I call," Nancy said.

She rejoined her friends and told them the discouraging news. Bess said, "Then this means, Nancy, that you're still in great danger."

The young sleuth smiled. "How could I be harmed with all of you around?"

When they arrived at the dig, the searchers found the young archaeologists jubilant. Art and Julie Anne together had unearthed the skeleton of a very important person.

"We think," said Theresa, "that he was probably the chief of the tribe. Others near him were no doubt his family and possibly they all were killed in a war. The chief's brain had been pierced by an arrow."

"How do you know he was the chief?" asked Dave.

"Because there was a fine antler headdress near his skull. Such a decoration was worn by an important man."

"This is exciting," Nancy said. "What a lot you did here today! I also have something for your exhibit." She took the spearheads from her pocket, and explained where they had been found.

"These are fine specimens," Theresa said. "I believe they're Hopewell work."

Nancy noticed that Bess had not waited to take part in the celebration. She had gone into the house immediately. Nancy and George headed for the cousins' room. Bess was not there.

"Let's find her," George proposed. She and Nancy went into the large old-fashioned kitchen. Bess, wearing a big apron, was preparing supper.

"I couldn't stand the sight of all those skeletons," she said.

The other two girls laughed and let Bess go on with her work while they went to change their clothes. Everyone enjoyed Bess's delicious supper of ham patties, macaroni and cheese, and banana ice cream topped with cherries and ground walnuts. Later all the boys left except Art. He had been elected to guard the lab that evening with its precious new collection from the excavation.

The girls lingered outside with Theresa to enjoy the balmy night air. Presently they became aware of a car coming up the road toward the farmhouse.

"Who can be calling at this time of night?" Theresa asked.

A camper was driven up. It stopped and two men in uniform stepped out and came toward the group.

One said, "We're guards from the museum in Cairo. We've come for all the artifacts and bones."

Nancy and the others stared at the men in astonishment.

CHAPTER XVI

Fakers

"Open the door to your laboratory!" the stranger ordered. "And any other place you keep artifacts the diggers found here."

Theresa stepped forward and asked for his credentials.

"What do you mean?" the other man said haughtily. "Our word is good enough."

Nancy was already suspicious of them and their mission. She quietly drew back among the girls and went over to the camper. In the moonlight she scraped the mud off the rear license plate and read the letters and numbers. She repeated them several times so she would not forget them, then returned to the group.

Theresa was still arguing with the men. One of them was saying, "Listen, lady, I could have this whole project stopped. Not one of you is from Illinois. You're trespassers!"

Theresa drew herself up very straight. "We have permission to work here," she said with dignity. "We certainly are not going to give you any of our finds."

By this time Art had come to Theresa's side.

"Want me to put these men off the place?" he asked, and added in a whisper, "With the girls' help we could do it."

Before Theresa had a chance to reply, the intruders started for the barn-lab. They were stopped short as the whole group moved toward them.

In a loud, clear voice Bess shouted, "If you dare try anything funny, George will use some judo on you!"

The men paused. Apparently they thought "George" was a man and they wanted no part of a judo encounter. Besides, Art was ready to fight them also. The two men looked from one to another in the group. Defeat in their eyes, they exchanged glances, then one said, "Okay for now. We'll leave but you can bet we'll be back!"

With this threat they walked to the camper and got in. Theresa, her students, and the visitors watched in relief as the vehicle pulled away.

When the chatter that followed died down, Nancy told Theresa that she had obtained the license number of the camper. "Would you like me to go with you to Walmsley now in Clem's truck and report the incident to the State Police?"

Theresa shook her head. "It might be dangerous. Those men were scared away because there were so many of us, but on the road they might waylay just two people. Wait until morning. Perhaps you and Ned could borrow Art's motorcycle and make the report. How about it, Art?"

"Glad to lend it," he said, and Nancy was delighted to see that he showed no sign of jealousy. Perhaps working closely with Julie Anne had made him realize what a fine girl she was and he was becoming more interested in her.

Theresa went on, "I'd ask you to go, Art, but you'll need some sleep after standing guard here."

"I understand," he replied.

The following morning Ned arrived driving the motorcycle, and after breakfast he and Nancy set off. When they arrived in town, she called State Police Headquarters and reported the incident of the previous night.

"I'm sure the men were phonies," she said. "I visited Cairo a short time ago. The only museum I know of is the Victorian mansion, and there were no uniformed guards. We were taken around by a woman guide."

The police captain agreed the men were impostors. "I'll alert my force to watch for them," he promised.

Nancy asked if any report had come in on Kit Kadle, alias Tom Wilson.

"Not a clue," he answered. "Did you say you

got the license number of the camper?" When Nancy gave it to him, he said, "Please stay there by that phone and I'll call you back. I'll get in touch with the license bureau and find out who owns the camper."

While she and Ned were waiting, Clem Rucker drove up in his car. He greeted them warmly and asked how they had made out the day before.

Nancy told him, then asked, "Do you know anything about that row of spearheads?"

The old farmer looked puzzled. "Never heard tell o' them. Where are they?" When he was told, he shook his head. "That sure is strange."

At that moment the telephone rang and Nancy answered. The State Police captain was calling back.

"That camper was stolen!" he reported.

The officer went on to say he had also checked with the museum in Cairo. They had not sent anybody to get artifacts or skeletons. "It was going to be a case of clear thievery but you and the young archaeologists foiled their scheme. My men will make a search and try to pick up those impostors."

While Nancy had been talking to the police, Ned had been telling Clem about the latest trouble at the dig.

"Somebody sure doesn't want you around here," the farmer remarked. "But pay no attention to 'em. You scared 'em all away before. You can do it again."

As Clem rode off, Nancy told Ned about the camper having been stolen and that the men who had driven to the dig were phonies.

Ned was thoughtful for a few seconds, then he said, "If those men who came to the dig last night are buddies of Kit Kadle, I'll bet he's in the area. I wonder if he moves around a lot, or has some particular place where he holes up."

"Wouldn't it be great to find his hideout?" Nancy asked.

"Big project," Ned answered.

He and Nancy mounted the motorcycle and it roared off toward the dig. At one point the road led through a rather thick copse. On a hunch Nancy asked Ned to slow down.

"Let's see if anybody is hiding in there," she proposed.

Ned cut down his speed while Nancy looked to left and right for signs of a trampled area. She not only could see one, but in the distance something shiny caught her eye.

"Ned!" she exclaimed. "Please stop!"

He brought the motorcycle to a halt, turned off the motor, and locked the engine.

"What is it?" he asked.

"Look there," Nancy said quietly, "among the trees."

"I see what you mean."

Ned insisted upon going first but told Nancy to stay close behind. As the couple advanced deep into the wooded area, they saw the stolen camper.

"You'd better stay out of sight while I investigate," Ned told Nancy. "If those thieves are around, they may try to harm you. They didn't see me last night so I could pretend I was just walking in here."

No one was in sight and a knock on the rear of the camper brought no response. Nancy climbed up to the driver's seat to see if she could find a clue.

"The keys are in the ignition," she called down. "Ned, we'd better take them and phone the police."

Ned agreed this was the thing to do. He pocketed the keys and the couple rode back to Walmsley. Nancy telephoned State Police Headquarters. The same officer whom she had talked to before answered.

"This is Nancy Drew again," she said. "I found the camper in a patch of woods about five miles outside of Walmsley. It's on the right going toward the dig."

The captain was astounded and said he would send two men over at once. "You and your friend had better wait in Walmsley and meet them."

The time went by quickly. When the officers arrived in a car, Nancy and Ned climbed aboard the motorcycle, and led the way to the hidden spot.

There was still no one around the camper. The troopers made a search for footprints but learned little.

Finally one said, "I'll drive this camper into town." He told his partner to take the police car. Nancy and Ned walked back to the road and went off on the motorcycle.

Everyone at the dig was eager to find out what they had learned about the intruders. The story amazed them.

Bess murmured, "To think that those horrible men were so near us all last night! Goodness only knows where they are now. Maybe very close!"

Burt and Dave as well as George had become intrigued with the art of digging. Theresa had explained to them how to go about it.

After lunch Nancy asked them if they would like to continue working there instead of searching for the hollow oak.

"Do you mind?" George spoke up.

"Of course not," she answered.

Bess wanted to make some special dessert for supper and begged to be excused from the sleuthing trip.

Julie Anne spoke up. "Art and I would love to go with you and Ned," she said. "He'll be here any minute."

Nancy said she thought this would be great. But deep in her heart she wondered if it would be. Or would a strained atmosphere develop? She did not reveal her thoughts and directly after lunch the four started off. Ned drove the old truck near the place where they had seen the spearheads.

"Wait here," Nancy requested. "I want to run down that incline and see if the spearheads are still there."

She found that they were, and was leaning more and more to the theory that Bob Snell had intended them to be a guide or signal. She returned to the others.

"Since the row points in an easterly direction, let's go that way to look for Bob," Nancy suggested.

Ned chuckled. "This is the end of our smooth ride," he told Julie Anne and Art. "From here on expect some bruises!"

He turned off the road, went down the incline, and through a field from which oats had been harvested. The truck bumped along. On the far side of the farmland Ned turned left around a patch of thick woods through which the vehicle could not go. Nancy spotted an overgrown footpath. The four young people climbed out of the truck and followed it.

Suddenly they emerged at the edge of a huge rocky pit. "It's an abandoned quarry," Ned remarked.

"And full of icky water," Julie Anne added.

Nancy was looking toward a sign near the far

end of the old quarry. She hurried over to see what it said. The words had been crudely painted. The young detective caught her breath as she read:

HOLLOW OAK AND ITS TREASURE AT
BOTTOM OF PIT

CHAPTER XVII

Unexpected Plunge

THE four searchers stared at the sign which had been stuck into the ground near the edge of the quarry.

"It can't be true," Ned said. "If anyone had found the treasure, why would he throw it into the water?"

They all gazed below. The water was murky and full of lime.

Art went over to examine the sign more closely. Presently he remarked that it looked newly painted.

"But by whom?" Julie Anne asked. "Nancy, what's your theory?"

"I have two," the young detective answered. "One is that the printing was done by Kit Kadle. He hoped that if I got this far, my search for the hollow oak would stop here. It means he must be somewhere in the vicinity."

"And what's your other theory?" Art queried.

"That when Bob Snell was kidnapped, he was brought past here and his abductors put up the sign to fool us so we wouldn't go looking for their hideout."

Nancy said she could not believe her search for Bob and for the hollow oak had ended in failure. "I'm going on farther to investigate!"

"But which way?" Ned asked.

While Nancy was thinking this over, the young people heard a crackling of twigs. Turning, they saw a huge dog bounding in their direction. Now he began to bark excitedly.

"He looks vicious!" Julie Anne exclaimed.

Everyone gazed around for a place to get out of his way. There was none. They had taken only a few steps when the great dog reached them. In a sudden lurch he leaped on Nancy. She lost her balance, stumbled backward, and fell into the quarry!

Julie Anne screamed. She and the boys watched, horror-stricken, as Nancy hit the water and disappeared.

Ned started down the steep embankment, while Art yanked a coil of wire from a pocket. Using it as a whip, he finally drove off the attacking dog. As it ran away, whimpering, Nancy's head appeared above the water.

"Oh, Nancy! Thank goodness!" cried Julie Anne. She was near tears.

"Are you all right?" Ned called down.

"Yes," Nancy replied. "Is everybody okay? Where's the dog?"

"Gone," Art answered.

"Good. As long as I'm here," Nancy said, treading water, "I'm going to investigate the bottom and see if by any chance there's a tree or part of one here." She swam around, diving now and then, but finally came to the side.

"There's nothing important down here," she reported.

Ned was at the edge of the water to assist her. She was a strange sight, dripping from head to foot with whitish water.

At once Ned pulled a handkerchief from his pocket. "Let me wipe off your eyes." He daubed at them, then the rest of her face, and pulled her up the embankment.

Julie Anne had noticed a little stream of clear water a short distance from the quarry and had hastened there to wet her own handkerchief. She ran back and applied it to Nancy's eyes, nose, and mouth. Then she burst out, "That dog ought to be tied up and never let loose!"

Nancy agreed but said, "We're probably trespassing on some farmer's property and the dog was only protecting it for his master."

Ned suggested that they go home. "Nancy, you should get out of those clothes and wash your hair as soon as possible."

*Dripping with whitish water, Nancy was
a strange sight*

She agreed. Her sopping wet attire was not only uncomfortable but gave her a strange whitish appearance.

"But we'll come back here tomorrow and continue our search for Bob," she told the others.

Meanwhile, Art had been walking around the edge of the quarry. Suddenly his foot kicked something. Leaning down, he picked up a metal object.

"Look!" he exclaimed. "Here's one of Père François's lead plates!"

The group concluded it probably had fallen off a tree, then had been picked up and later dropped at this point. But who had dropped it and when? There was no way of finding out the direction in which the arrow had once pointed.

"We'll have to search in all directions at once," Nancy said ruefully.

Art put it into his pocket and they all trekked back to the truck. On the way to the dig, Nancy reflected upon the friendliness and cooperation of Julie Anne, Art, and Ned. Outside of Nancy's accident, everything had been most cordial and pleasant.

"Now I won't have to worry any more about jealousy and tense moments," she told herself, smiling in relief.

As the group stepped from the truck at the farmhouse, some of the girls were just coming in from the dig. They stared at Nancy with her white hair and clothing.

"What in the world happened to you?" asked one of them.

Nancy laughed. "Believe it or not, I fell into a quarry pit. And now I'm going in for a good bath and a shampoo, then wash these clothes."

Bess, who had come from the kitchen, stared at her friend in disbelief. She at once offered to take care of Nancy's clothes.

An hour later Nancy emerged from the farm-house in a clean pants outfit, with her hair back to its natural reddish-blond color. Meeting Theresa, she told her about the sign and her suspicion that the kidnappers' hideout might be near the quarry.

They were interrupted by George who was just coming from the excavation. She was obviously excited.

"See what I dug up!" she exclaimed, exhibiting a tray of sand in which there was a circle of tiny river pearls. "These were probably once a necklace," she explained.

Theresa examined them. "This is an important find."

Bess had come out of the house in time to hear George's remark.

"You mean," she said, "that there was once a neck inside of those pearls?"

Nancy and George laughed. George could not resist teasing her cousin. "That's right. The lady's head and neck were dug up first."

"Ugh! How can you enjoy such gruesome

things?" Bess remarked, and returned to the kitchen.

That evening after dinner the young people gathered in the living room. It had grown chilly outside and the logs in the fireplace were lighted. The farmhouse did not have a television set, but there was a good radio.

"Let's see if we can get some news," Theresa said. "I've been so engrossed here it's high time I caught up with what's going on in the outside world."

She turned on the set. The newscaster was telling about an earthquake in Peru and the resignation of a college president. A commercial followed.

When it was finished, the announcer said, "This station has just received a message from a ham radio operator. It may be a hoax. We cannot guarantee its authenticity but we give it to you in case you may know the person involved. The ham picked up the following broadcast:

" '*I'm Bob Snell. Repeat. I'm Bob Snell. I'm well but a prisoner at—*'

"That was all the ham heard," the announcer concluded.

There was another short commercial, then the regular newscast was continued. The young people in the farmhouse were electrified by what they had heard.

"Oh, I hope they tell more!" Nancy said excitedly.

To the dismay of the group the announcer did not mention the ham's message again. They assumed the police had picked it up and would investigate.

Theresa spoke up. "This is both good news and bad news. It confirms our fears that Bob was kidnapped, but it's a good lead for the authorities to work on."

"And for us too," Nancy told her with determination.

CHAPTER XVIII

Well-House Clue

THE farmhouse radio was kept on. The group hoped for further word of Bob Snell which the ham operator might have sent. Over an hour passed and there was no mention of him.

"This is nerve-racking," Bess murmured.

"*Sh!*" George warned.

Just then another news flash came on about the missing young man. The ham operator had reported he thought the prisoner must be a ham himself and had managed to rig up a sending set.

"But no doubt he was interrupted and his gear taken away from him," the announcer said.

This was the end of the news flash.

"Bob *is* a ham," Todd Smith spoke up. "He fools around with short-wave radio all the time."

"Then," Ned said, "we can be pretty sure the message was genuine." He turned to Nancy. "What do you think we should do about this?"

"I'm afraid," she said, "the abductors will move

Bob before the police can track down the spot from which he beamed his message."

Art and Todd offered to ride to town on the motorcycle and telephone the police for news.

Nancy said, "How about calling the radio station and the ham? Maybe you'll learn more."

"We'll do that," Art promised.

When the group heard the motorcycle coming back, everyone rushed outdoors. "What did you find out?" several of them asked.

"I got in touch with the ham," Art answered. "He thinks Bob beamed his message from somewhere in southern Illinois in an open area."

"That's where we are!" Julie Anne exclaimed.

Theresa said, "I suggest a day off tomorrow so most of you can try to find Bob. I will stay here with four others to guard our dig and the lab."

The young archaeologists planned to start out early the next morning, dividing the territory. Nancy thought that her group should go back to the quarry and start from there.

Good-nights were being said when they became aware of an old car driving in. As soon as it stopped, Clem Rucker stepped out.

"Howdy, folks," he greeted everyone. "I was in town this evenin' and picked up a letter for you, Nancy, in my box. Funny thing, it was mailed right in Walmsley yesterday. Must be from somebody you know around here."

Since the young detective knew no one in the

area except Roscoe Thompson and this was not his handwriting, her curiosity was aroused. She tore open the letter and glanced through it. A frown creased her forehead. She read aloud:

" 'Bob Snell is our prisoner. We will release him after you give us the contents of the hollow oak plus five thousand dollars. Leave them tomorrow morning before seven o'clock in the abandoned well house one mile west of the quarry. Do not notify the police or you will regret it.' The note is not signed."

"Oh!" Julie Anne exclaimed. "This is dreadful!"

"Now we really have something to work on," George remarked. Nancy nodded.

Julie Anne said, "Nancy, surely you aren't going to give those abductors five thousand dollars!"

"Of course not. Even if I could, I wouldn't." She suggested that they leave a dummy sack containing paper and a few stones in the well house.

At once Claire Warwick spoke up. "I'm sure the whole thing will be a wild-goose chase. Nothing has convinced me that Bob was really abducted. He probably is just playing a joke on us. You're wasting your time. It is more important to stay here and dig."

With that she went into the farmhouse without saying good night to anyone.

Bess turned to Nancy. "You don't think there could be any truth in her conclusion, do you?"

"No," Nancy replied. "Bob wouldn't play such an idiotic joke."

"That's right," Art added. "He's too nice a guy to worry his parents and friends."

"We must get this note to the police," said Theresa, and Nancy agreed, despite the warning against doing so.

"I'll run you down to State Police Headquarters on the highway," said Clem. "Hop in."

Nancy, Ned, and Theresa accepted his offer and thirty minutes later the four were seated before the desk of a brisk young police captain. He studied the note carefully, then listened intently to Nancy's plan about leaving the dummy sack.

"This ransom note could be a hoax," he said, "but we'll check it. Miss Drew, I think that you and your friends should deliver the sack as you suggested. I'll keep my men hidden in the woods. If the kidnappers think the police are around they won't go through with the deal."

The details were arranged and everyone agreed, though Theresa was concerned about the danger.

"Don't worry," Nancy said confidently. "We'll be cautious."

Next morning everybody was up very early. Nancy and her friends from home ate a quick breakfast, then piled into the truck, taking the dummy sack which the boys had fixed the night before. The others waved good-by and called, "Good luck!"

A short distance from the quarry, Ned parked the truck. Then the three couples headed in a westerly direction. Burt and George walked a little to the left of Nancy and Ned, while Dave and Bess went to the right.

The instructions in the letter proved to be correct. Exactly one mile from the quarry they came upon an old well house. It had originally been part of a farm home but now there were only ruins of a burned house and barn.

"The abductors certainly chose a secluded spot for the ransom," Nancy said.

She and Ned hurried forward. The other two couples watched from a distance, then they all converged. Cautiously Nancy and Ned led the way to the small, shadowy well house. It was empty. As Ned laid down the sack of paper and stones, Nancy looked around. On the far side she noticed a crumpled paper on the floor. Nancy picked it up to see if anything was on it.

"A message from Bob!" she cried. "Listen! 'Was a prisoner here but am being moved. I don't know where. Hollow oak not located.' "

"What a find!" Ned exclaimed. "I wonder how long ago he wrote this."

"Let's hope," George put in, "that we're so hot on the trail, those kidnappers haven't been able to take Bob far away."

Everyone was excited and now began to hunt

outside for clues to the direction the kidnappers had gone. Dave was the first to spot two sets of footprints leading in a northeasterly direction. Did the prints belong to two abductors who might have been carrying Bob, or to Bob and one abductor?

"I believe one set is Bob's," Nancy remarked.

"We must follow them, of course," said Ned, "but somebody ought to stay here and stake out the well house."

George and Burt volunteered to keep watch. "I'll bark like a dog," said Burt, "if the kidnappers show up."

"Okay," Ned replied. "Besides, you'll be safe enough because the police are supposed to be hiding around here." He frowned. "They're doing a good job, if they are. There's not a sign of them."

Nancy set off with her friends. A short distance away the footprints ended but tire tracks took their place. The two couples followed them. The marks went straight for some distance, then curved abruptly around a hill.

Not knowing what might confront them on the other side of it, the four young people went ahead cautiously, single file. Ned had insisted upon taking the lead in case there was any trouble. When they reached the far side, they saw an empty car parked in a clearing.

On a hunch that someone would soon come for it, Nancy suggested, "Let's retrace our steps and spy around the side of the hill."

In a few minutes their caution was rewarded. They could hear voices. Soon three men approached on foot. The watchers gasped.

In the center was Bob Snell, blindfolded and gagged!

On either side of him were the fake museum guards who had come to the farmhouse.

"Don't try any funny work, young man!" one of them said in a harsh voice.

The watchers looked at one another, then got ready to attack!

CHAPTER XIX

Surprise!

THE fake guards were taken completely by surprise. Ned and Dave gave them a football rush that knocked the two men over.

For a few seconds Bob did not know what was going on. He put up his fists to ward off anyone who might attack him. Instantly Nancy and Bess came to his rescue. Quickly they untied his blindfold and pulled the gag from his mouth.

"Nancy!" Bob cried out. "Where did you come from?"

Without waiting for an answer he pitched into the fight to help Ned and Dave. The kidnappers were quickly subdued. Exhausted, they did not try to escape.

Nancy introduced her friends to Bob. He thanked them for rescuing him, and said, "How did you ever find me?"

Nancy explained and added, "Oh, Bob, we're so glad to see you!"

He managed a smile. "Am I glad to see you! How's everything at the dig?"

Quickly Nancy told about the attempted thievery, then asked, "Who kidnapped you?"

Bob confirmed that it was Kit Kadle. "By the way, he does use the alias of Tom Wilson."

Nancy quizzed the prisoners, but they sat on the ground, looking glum and refusing to answer. Bob said he did not know their names but the men were pals of Kit Kadle.

"Did you hear the radio message I sent that a ham picked up? Evidently he passed it on."

"Yes, to a broadcasting company," Nancy replied. "Later we learned the ham thought you were in this general area."

Just then George and Burt came around the side of the hill. They stopped short at the surprising scene before them, then hurried over, full of questions.

Swiftly Ned explained the situation and Nancy introduced the newcomers to Bob. Then she turned to George. "Why did you leave the well house?"

"Because the police have the well house surrounded. One of the officers spotted us and said it wasn't necessary for us to keep watch. We came to see if you needed our help."

Bob nodded. "How about tying up these men?

There's some rope in that car of theirs, and by the way, the ignition key is in it."

The two prisoners suddenly tried to make a break, but they were quickly stopped by the four boys. Since it seemed best for all of them to hold onto the men, George went to the car and found the rope. She helped tie the men's hands behind their backs and hobbled their feet.

The prisoners sat down again, glaring at their captors. Burt offered to bring back a couple of policemen who were staking out the well house.

While Burt was gone, Bob explained how he had been kidnapped. "It happened while I was near the dig," he said. "These two guys came out of nowhere. While one of them stuffed a gag in my mouth, the other one grabbed me and tore my shirt. A piece of it came off in my hand when I tried reaching for the guy's arm. Before they had a chance to tie me up, I pretended to pass out. I staggered toward a tree and stuck the material in it. They dragged me away and made me walk in a brook a long distance. The whole time I kept wondering what my capture was all about.

"Later I found out Kit Kadle was in back of the whole thing. He was very nervous about being found, so he had these men moving me from place to place in their car. They had another car they had stolen but were afraid to use it.

"I told them I didn't know anything about the hollow oak, but they didn't believe me. Kadle figured that the message contained directions to a hidden treasure. If he could find it, he would be a rich man. And I guess he also planned to sell whatever he could steal from the dig."

George said, "We found the note you left in the well house. Did they keep you a prisoner there part of the time?"

"Yes," Bob replied. "One or the other of the two armed guards always kept watch outside the places where Kadle and I stayed. Kadle was away a lot, so I had plenty of time to try figuring out how I could save myself."

Nancy was curious about the strange row of stones she had found. "Did you leave them?"

"Yes. When the men took me out for exercise, they untied my hands. I spotted the spearheads in a heap. While they were busy talking, I filled my pockets with them. Later, they moved me. When they weren't watching me for a few seconds, I dropped the spearheads onto the ground one by one. Once I tried to get away but it was hopeless."

Bess spoke up. "I think you were marvelous to rig up a sending set and get a message out. Where did you find the equipment?"

Bob laughed. "I'm studying to be an electrical engineer, and you'd be surprised at all the odd little things I gathered in that shack where Kadle was staying. I worked on the set whenever he was out."

"Where is this shack?" Nancy asked.

"I don't know," Bob replied. "In the woods somewhere. I was blindfolded whenever they moved me in and out of it."

"Is he at the place now?" asked Ned.

Bob said Kadle had gone off somewhere but had told the men he would join them later.

"In the meantime they were to move me to a new hideout. Kadle caught me sending the radio message last night and figured the police would soon locate the place where we were staying."

"When is he going to the well house to pick up the ransom?" Nancy asked.

"Sometime this morning," Bob replied. "That's all I know. Nancy, did you find the message in the hollow oak?"

"No," she said, "but apparently Kadle thinks I did, because he made it part of the ransom."

Bob shook his head. "Kadle doesn't know whether you have or haven't. He just put that in the ransom note in case you had. Anyway, he figures he'll get five thousand dollars."

Ned grinned. "Is he in for a surprise!" Bob laughed when he was told about the dummy sack.

Ned turned to the prisoners and questioned them about where they had planned to take Bob. The men remained silent.

"It doesn't matter now, anyway," said Nancy. "The police should be here soon."

To her dismay Burt returned without them,

saying he could not find any of the officers. "I figure they either captured Kadle or are trailing him."

After a discussion it was decided that Bob and Burt would use the prisoners' car and take the kidnappers to the authorities.

"Bob, please don't go before you answer a few more questions," Nancy requested. "Did you ever find out why you were abducted?"

"Yes," Bob replied. "Two reasons. One, Kadle hoped my disappearance would frighten you off the case. Two, he thought I could give him a clue to the hollow oak. He was sure I had picked up information about it from you."

"How did he learn the story of the oak?" Nancy asked.

"He overheard the New York detectives talking about it when they were out here," Bob answered.

Nancy asked him if he knew one of those detectives had been kidnapped by Kadle. "No. But I'm not surprised. Kadle is a fanatic on the subject of the hollow oak. He's determined to find it first and won't let anything stand in his way.

"I'd say," Bob went on, "that because you found both Mr. Armstrong and myself, Kadle will pretty nearly go berserk. Nancy, I'm afraid you are in serious danger."

The young detective brushed off the idea. She whispered to Bob, "Did you pick up any clues about a hollow oak?"

"Maybe," he replied. "I did see something that the men didn't notice. About two hundred feet beyond the open field there's a giant oak. I don't know if it's hollow, but there's a tremendous lump on the trunk. Perhaps something is underneath it."

Ned remarked in a concerned tone, "I think the quicker we get these prisoners to State Police Headquarters the better."

The other young people agreed he was right. Bob and Burt started off with their captives.

After they had gone, Nancy and her friends hurried across the open field and found the oak tree easily. There was indeed a good-sized hump on the trunk, but the tree was not hollow.

Ned brought out his hunting knife and chipped off the bark over the lump. The others watched intently. Finally his efforts were rewarded.

"Here's a lead plate," he said, and pried it loose. After he had cleaned it off, the initials P.F. were revealed. This was followed by an arrow pointing directly north.

Bess sighed. "Père François certainly must have traveled around to many Indian villages. When are we going to come to the end of our search?"

"Good question," George replied. "Well, let's head north!"

The five friends walked along silently, watching for a hollow oak. After a while they heard the sound of a waterfall. In a few minutes they arrived at the edge of a steep embankment. It led down to a rushing stream which tumbled over a rock ledge. In the wet and shadowy depths under the falls Nancy saw something which made her heart beat faster.

"Look!" she exclaimed. "There's an oak tree wedged under that waterfall. It's being held in place by rocks."

"Great!" Dave remarked and added, "Here's the stump on the embankment. The tree must have rotted, then been blown over by a heavy wind. It rolled down into the stream."

The whole group was excited now. They realized that if the mammoth tree was rotten at the stump, it no doubt was hollow all the way through.

"I'm going down to investigate," Nancy announced.

"Not without me," Ned said firmly.

He took her arm and the two started down the slippery embankment. A moment later the earth gave way. The couple lost their footing and slid toward the water.

"Oh!" Bess screamed above them.

Nancy and Ned managed to break their fall just before reaching the rocky stream. Now they stood up and gazed at the giant oak which reached from bank to bank. They leaned down and peered through a hole in it. The tree was indeed hollow.

"Could this be the real hollow oak?" Nancy asked excitedly.

"Let's inspect it!" Ned urged.

The two waded into the stream and examined the bark. Nancy hoped fervently that if there were a hump indicating an object underneath, it would not be on the underside of the tree.

"Here's something!" she called out in a few moments.

George shouted down, "What do you think?"

"Tell you in a moment," Ned replied. "Dave, did you bring along your little hatchet?"

"I sure did," Dave replied.

He came down the embankment cautiously. George and Bess stayed at the top and kept looking around them to see if anyone were watching. If Kadle had not been captured and were in the neighborhood he would surely try to interfere.

Using the hatchet, Dave soon uncovered another name plate. On it were the initials P.F. but there was no arrow!

"We've found it! We've found it!" Nancy cried gleefully.

The tree was quite rotted. The young people figured it could not have been in the water very long, or it would have fallen apart. After a few gentle whacks with the hatchet they came to the hollow section.

"Oh!" Nancy murmured.

Inside lay a long, narrow metal box. Ned lifted it out, then the elated finders started up the embankment with it.

"I can't believe it!" Bess called down. "You've found the treasure!"

Nancy was almost too excited to speak. She could hardly wait to see what was in the box. Because of its size and weight she realized there must be something more inside than just the message. The metal box was laid on the ground at the top of the embankment and brushed off.

"Here are Père François's initials." George pointed.

There was a lock but no key. The metal had rusted, however, and with little effort Ned pried the lid open. In the box lay a copper hunting horn decorated with exquisite Limoges porcelain work depicting scenes in France.

"It's beautiful," said Bess as Nancy lifted the horn from the box.

"The message must be hidden inside!" she exclaimed.

Nancy was about to put her hand into the horn when a voice near the group commanded:

"Hand that over to me!"

CHAPTER XX

Kit and Caboodle

NANCY and her friends whirled to see who had ordered her to hand over the treasure.

Kadle! Beside him stood a man with a gun.

Nancy's heart sank. After all her hard work, was she going to have to surrender her discovery to a thief? Defiantly she asked, "Why should I give this to you?"

"Never mind the reason!" Kadle shouted angrily. "Come here, all of you!"

Bess, trembling, started to walk ahead. Dave stepped to her side.

The next moment Nancy, Ned, and George spotted two state troopers hurrying toward them among the trees. The three friends exchanged looks. Then, playing for time, Nancy continued to oppose Kadle.

"What would you do with this?" she asked. "And how much would you pay for it?"

"Don't be ridiculous!" Kadle shouted, stepping forward a pace.

Bess turned her head. "You'd better do as he says, Nancy. We don't want to get hurt."

"She's right!" Kadle called out.

Before he could move again, the troopers sprang from the woods and seized the two men.

"Hey! What's going on here?" Kadle sputtered. The man with him looked thunderstruck at being disarmed.

One of the troopers said, "We've been looking for you a long time. You're wanted on several counts and now we can add to the list threatening the lives of these young people."

"It's a lie!" Kadle blustered. He pointed to Nancy. "She has something that belongs to me!"

The trooper asked Nancy, "Is this true?"

"Of course not," she replied. "I'd say that if this property belongs to anyone, it would be the State of Illinois. I promise to turn it in." She told the officers a little of the mystery on which she was working.

"It's lucky you arrived when you did," Ned said to the troopers. "How did you find us? Did our friends tell you?"

"No, we haven't seen them."

"They've taken the phony guards to jail." Kadle winced at hearing this.

The trooper went on, "We were hiding near the well house, and spotted you going through the woods. A few minutes later Kadle and his pal came along, following you. We trailed them, figuring we'd catch the two in action."

Ned turned to Kadle. "Then you never did go to the well house to pick up the ransom?"

Kadle shook his head. "When I noticed you heading in this direction, I was sure you were up to something and I'd better find out what it was."

Dave said, "There was a nice fat sack of paper and stones waiting for you at the well house."

Kadle scowled. "I might have known Nancy Drew would pull a trick on me."

Seeing that his position was hopeless, he talked freely. Nancy learned the answers to some of the questions which had puzzled her. The two men who had later posed as museum guards had come to the dig soon after her arrival and called out her name softly at the bedroom window. They were supposed to get Nancy to step outside and then kidnap her, so she could not pursue her search for the message in the hollow oak. The men had also stolen Clem's goat to frighten her in the dark bedroom.

"But nothing worked," Kadle admitted.

One of his men left the note on the farmhouse bureau, hoping to scare Nancy off the case. Kadle had planned to steal the fossils and artifacts in the excavation and the barn, and admitted posing as Tom Wilson.

"Whenever I thought it wasn't safe for me to appear, I gave the job to my men."

Nancy asked, "Did you mutilate an oak tree in your search for the real hollow oak?"

Kadle admitted doing it.

George spoke up. "How did you learn Nancy Drew was on the case?"

Kadle replied, "When I couldn't get any information from Armstrong about the hollow oak, I flew East and spied on the other detectives. I overheard Boycey Osborne say Nancy Drew from River Heights was taking over. I managed to get on the same flight with her to St. Louis."

The trooper asked if the prisoners had any more to say. They shook their heads and were led away.

"Now let's see what's inside this hunting horn," Nancy suggested.

While Ned held the beautiful instrument, she put her hand down inside the tube. Her fingers touched something metal. She pulled out a heavy solid-gold chain and cross.

"That's exquisite!" Bess exclaimed.

"And worth a fortune, I'll bet," Dave added.

Next Nancy removed a man's large signet ring with a religious design on it. She tugged at the next piece but could not move it.

Finally she said, "Ned, you try."

The object was wedged in tightly. Ned rocked the horn from side to side and finally the metal object in it gave way. He pulled out a slender brass box.

"This is a surveyor's kit," Dave remarked as Nancy raised the lid. "Père François must have been a surveyor as well as a missionary."

Carefully Nancy removed an egg-shaped piece of metal with a rotted fragment of string attached to it.

"That's a plumb bob," said Ned. "It hangs on the end of a line to find the center of gravity."

"And here's a compass," George added.

"What's this?" Nancy asked, picking up a brass tube.

"Père François could have used that for sighting," said Ned. "Today we look through a telescopic instrument called a transit."

Nancy slid her finger into the tube. "Something's in here!" she exclaimed, and pulled out a tiny roll of paper. "It must be the message that tells about the treasure!"

The handwriting on the paper proved to be in French and some of the words were old-fashioned, but Nancy managed to translate them. She read aloud:

" 'This tree is quarter of a mile east from an ancient Indian burial mound. It is large, overgrown, and the rounded top is gone. I dug into it from the side and found fine objects. Then war came. I put them back and filled in the hole.

" 'The Iroquois are destroying the Algonquin. The last village I was in was attacked and I fled, but the arrow wound I received is festering and I shall die. I will hide my few precious possessions in this hollow oak. Then I will put a note in a light crock, seal it, and send it downstream. I pray the note will be picked up by a settler. These belongings were brought by me from France to New France.' "

As Nancy paused, George remarked, "New France is now Canada, isn't it?"

"Yes," Nancy answered, then went on reading:

" 'I have marked my journey from one Indian village to another by placing lead plates I brought from France upon oak trees near Indian settlements. Arrows I made on the signs show the direction of my travels. One plate is left which has no arrow. I will use it to mark this tree.' "

The young people stood silent, awed by what they had just seen and learned.

Finally Ned said, "Nancy, I don't think you realize what a tremendous find you've made."

The young detective merely smiled. "Evidently someone found the crock with the note, and the story became a legend."

George patted her friend on the back. "And then Nancy Drew turned the legend into a true story."

Carrying the copper box with the fabulous

hunting horn with them, Nancy and her friends returned to the farmhouse. As the truck clattered in, Theresa and the young archaeologists began appearing from all directions to find out what their friends had learned.

"It must have been a good day," said Julie Anne. "You're all smiling!"

Nancy jumped down and said, "My smile is as wide as the Illinois river country." She told of their finding Bob and the capture of Kadle and his pals.

"How marvelous!" Julie Anne exclaimed.

Ned and Dave now lifted down the copper box. Nancy opened it and displayed the beautiful hunting horn.

The first one to speak up was Claire Warwick. "What kind of a message is that?"

The others ignored her and asked Nancy to show them the other treasures. Finally she came to the note and once more translated it.

"You have done an amazing job, Nancy," said Theresa. "As for that burial mound, I can't wait to see it!"

She determined that as soon as the present dig site had been thoroughly excavated, she would ask for permission to work on the new one.

All the young people said they would like to join in the expedition. Todd remarked, "I doubt that what we'll find will be as valuable as this hunting horn."

"But much older," Julie Anne reminded him. She was standing very close to Art and from the looks they were exchanging Nancy was sure they were now very good friends.

"We have a surprise for you, Nancy," Art said. "We found the rest of the baby's skeleton that matched the fingers and forearm you unearthed."

"Great!" Nancy said. "And thanks for finishing my job."

Bess gave a little shudder. "I'm glad I wasn't here when you brought it up. The poor little baby!"

A short time later Burt and Bob arrived in a state trooper's car. A rousing cheer went up for Bob. When the acclaim subsided, the boys reported that the two fake guards were in jail.

"I called my parents," said Bob. "Nancy, they're very grateful to you and your friends for rescuing me. And I am, too."

He and Burt were told of the capture of Kadle and his companion.

"That's a relief," said Bob. "I never want to be kidnapped again!"

Stories were exchanged by diggers, treasure hunters, and Bob Snell. It seemed unbelievable that so many things had occurred during one morning.

Nancy had a suggestion. "Let's ask the state for permission to donate the lead plates to Paulson University."

Theresa smiled. "They'll be delighted to receive them."

That evening after supper Nancy said, "Since it's a beautiful clear night and there are no longer kidnappers or thieves around, I'd like to go to town and phone my father, my Aunt Eloise, and Boycey Osborne."

Art offered his motorcycle to her and Ned.

"And we should stop and tell Clem," Nancy said.

When she telephoned Boycey Osborne, he was so amazed he almost lost his voice. "You've actually tracked down the message in the hollow oak and found a treasure!" he exclaimed. "Well my congratulations, Nancy. And please stay at the dig until I come out and see everything. To tell the truth, I'm very much embarrassed that my friends and I weren't able to solve this mystery!"

"All you needed was more time," Nancy told him kindly. "Now that my work here is finished, I'll have to get home. When can you come?"

"I'll take a plane tonight," was the quick answer.

Mr. Drew, Hannah Gruen, and Aunt Eloise were equally amazed. All praised the young detective, but she insisted that her friends deserved a great deal of credit for solving the mystery.

On the way back to the dig, Nancy and Ned stopped at Clem's house. The old farmer's astonishment was immense. He thumped his thighs and danced around with as much glee as if he had found the message and treasure himself.

"That beats all!" he said. "I'll be up tomorrow mornin' to see that there huntin' horn. You folks sure brought excitement to this place. We haven't had so much goin' on around here since one o' the town girls eloped with the postmaster's son."

Embarrassed by Clem's comment, Nancy and Ned smiled.

By noontime the next day the farmhouse and yard were full of visitors. Not only were Clem and his wife there, but Mr. Drew, Aunt Eloise, and all the members of the New York Detective Club! Nancy blushed at the praise showered on her.

"Nancy, after a meeting with my friends, we voted unanimously to make you an honorary member of our club!"

For a moment Nancy felt like crying, but she regained her composure and thanked them all.

"This is a marvelous honor," she said, then chuckled. With a wink at Boycey Osborne, she said, "Any time I can help you on such a fascinating mystery as this one, let me know." Everyone laughed and applauded.

Nancy's next case did not come through Boycey, but it proved to be a particularly intriguing one called, *Mystery of the Ivory Charm.*

Theresa now stepped forward and put one hand on Nancy's shoulder. "I hurried into town this morning," she said, "and made some phone calls.

I have permission from the property owner to dig the mound discovered by Père François. It is probably a Hopewell burial. Paulson University has promised to finance the expedition and I am to lead it. Nancy, I want you to have the honor of digging the first shovelful of dirt."

Again everyone clapped and Nancy gave Theresa a hug and whispered, "I'll never forget this wonderful experience as long as I live!"

Postscript

The Hopewell mound was excavated the following summer and found to contain many perfectly preserved artifacts and fossils, including several bird effigies in stone, and a rare baby's cradle. At a luncheon celebration which followed the event, Nancy was praised for having added valuable information to the archaeological knowledge of America.

With a smile she said, "All the credit belongs to Père François and his message in the hollow oak."

ORDER FORM

NANCY DREW MYSTERY SERIES

Now that you've met Nancy Drew and her friends, we're sure you'll want to "accompany" them on other exciting adventures. So for your convenience, we've enclosed this handy order form.

54 TITLES AT YOUR BOOKSELLER
OR COMPLETE AND MAIL THIS
HANDY COUPON TO:

GROSSET & DUNLAP, INC.
P.O. Box 941, Madison Square Post Office, New York, N.Y. 10010

Please send me the Nancy Drew Mystery Book(s) checked below @ $2.50 each, plus 25¢ *per book* postage and handling. My check or money order for $_____ is enclosed.

☐	1. Secret of the Old Clock	9501-7	☐	27. Secret of the Wooden Lady	9527-0
☐	2. Hidden Staircase	9502-5	☐	28. The Clue of the Black Keys	9528-9
☐	3. Bungalow Mystery	9503-3	☐	29. Mystery at the Ski Jump	9529-7
☐	4. Mystery at Lilac Inn	9504-1	☐	30. Clue of the Velvet Mask	9530-0
☐	5. Secret of Shadow Ranch	9505-X	☐	31. Ringmaster's Secret	9531-9
☐	6. Secret of Red Gate Farm	9506-8	☐	32. Scarlet Slipper Mystery	9532-7
☐	7. Clue in the Diary	9507-6	☐	33. Witch Tree Symbol	9533-5
☐	8. Nancy's Mysterious Letter	9508-4	☐	34. Hidden Window Mystery	9534-3
☐	9. The Sign of the Twisted Candles	9509-2	☐	35. Haunted Showboat	9535-1
☐	10. Password to Larkspur Lane	9510-6	☐	36. Secret of the Golden Pavilion	9536-X
☐	11. Clue of the Broken Locket	9511-4	☐	37. Clue in the Old Stagecoach	9537-8
☐	12. The Message in the Hollow Oak	9512-2	☐	38. Mystery of the Fire Dragon	9538-6
☐	13. Mystery of the Ivory Charm	9513-0	☐	39. Clue of the Dancing Puppet	9539-4
☐	14. The Whispering Statue	9514-9	☐	40. Moonstone Castle Mystery	9540-8
☐	15. Haunted Bridge	9515-7	☐	41. Clue of the Whistling Bagpipes	9541-6
☐	16. Clue of the Tapping Heels	9516-5	☐	42. Phantom of Pine Hill	9542-4
☐	17. Mystery of the Brass Bound Trunk	9517-3	☐	43. Mystery of the 99 Steps	9543-2
☐	18. Mystery at Moss-Covered Mansion	9518-1	☐	44. Clue in the Crossword Cipher	9544-0
☐	19. Quest of the Missing Map	9519-X	☐	45. Spider Sapphire Mystery	9545-9
☐	20. Clue in the Jewel Box	9520-3	☐	46. The Invisible Intruder	9546-7
☐	21. The Secret in the Old Attic	9521-1	☐	47. The Mysterious Mannequin	9547-5
☐	22. Clue in the Crumbling Wall	9522-X	☐	48. The Crooked Banister	9548-3
☐	23. Mystery of the Tolling Bell	9523-8	☐	49. The Secret of Mirror Bay	9549-1
☐	24. Clue in the Old Album	9524-6	☐	50. The Double Jinx Mystery	9550-5
☐	25. Ghost of Blackwood Hall	9525-4	☐	51. Mystery of the Glowing Eye	9551-3
☐	26. Clue of the Leaning Chimney	9526-2	☐	52. The Secret of the Forgotten City	9552-1
			☐	53. The Sky Phantom	9553-X
			☐	54. The Strange Message in the Parchment	9554-1

SHIP TO:

NAME _____
(please print)

ADDRESS _____

CITY _____ STATE _____ ZIP _____